Who's Your Daddy?

Bible-Based Stories
Showing God As
A Father for Us All

DAVID R. NELSON

NASHVILLE
NEW YORK • LONDON • MELBOURNE • VANCOUVER

Who's Your Daddy?

Bible-Based Stories Showing God As A Father for Us All

Published in New York, New York, by Morgan James Publishing. Morgan James is a trademark of Morgan James, LLC. www.MorganJamesPublishing.com

The Morgan James Speakers Group can bring authors to your live event. For more information or to book an event visit The Morgan James Speakers Group at www.TheMorganJamesSpeakersGroup.com.

This is a work of fiction. All of the characters, names, incidents, organizations, and dialogue in this novel are either the products of the author's imagination or are used fictitiously.

ISBN 9781642790412 paperback
ISBN 9781642790429 eBook
Library of Congress Control Number: 2018903580

Cover Design by:
Megan Dillon
megan@creativeninjadesigns.com

Interior Design by:
Christopher Kirk
http://GFSstudio.com

"The approach reminds me of some of the material that I have read of Max Lucado. Reading together as a family would, I'm sure, be a real conversation starter - probably the strength of the book. Even also in sermon/bible study/ Sunday school prep it would be a good thought promoter. A book of this type, I think has a particular … appeal."

Steven Bowes
Mission Director, European Mission Fellowship:

"It is always good to help people to reconnect with the stories which have shaped their culture. The Bible has had a huge influence on the life of the United Kingdom, but in the twenty-first century it is often little known and poorly understood. We need imaginative ways of bringing it once more to the centre of our communities and families, so that it can help once more to give people the sense of meaning and purpose for which we all hunger. David Nelson's work in his telling of Bible-based stories is to be warmly encouraged for this reason."

Revd. Stephen I. Wright BA, BA, MA, PhD
Vice Principal - Academic Director, Spurgeon's College:

"My understanding of the book's origin has led me to conclude that these stories are inspired from the throne room of heaven."

Dr. Mark A Minott
FCollT, FHERDSA, .EdD, MSc,
PGDE, DipHE, AT Dip, CJSM (Cr), TTC

To Lorna, Da'lano, and Jordan
Mom and Dad
My Family
Pastor Dudley McKenzie, Elder Leabert, and Joy Todd
and the fellowship at Lyndhurst Gospel Assembly, JA
My friends at Brixton and Roundwood Gospel Assemblies, UK.

My lifetime friend and brother Dr. Mark Anthony Minott,
Auntie would be proud.

I would like to say a special thank you to
Ms. Diana Gittens for her commentary and
Dr. Jennifer Williams for her encouragement and guidance.

Finally, I want to thank the team at Morgan James Publishing.
A special thank you to David Hancock, CEO & Founder.
To my Managing Editor, Gayle West, thank you for making the process seamless and easy. Many more thanks to everyone else, but especially Jim Howard, Bethany Marshall, and Aubrey Kosa.
I would also like to thank Terry Whalin who believed in my work and introduced me to the Morgan James family.
You all have offered great support and encouragement.

Contents

Foreword

Stories are valued because they effectively engage our imagination, illustrate deeper meaning, and give us insight into life. This is true of the stories included in *Who's Your Daddy? Bible Based Stories Showing God As A Father for Us All.* They not only help us to imagine what situations must have been like for the familiar Bible characters, but they also demonstrate God's involvement in our lives. Most significantly, they point us to the father-child relationship we have with God, they encourage us to trust Him and depend on His fatherly love and care, and they remind us of the desirability of having childlike trust in our Father.

While reading *Who's Your Daddy*? I constantly reflected on the nature and character of God. What is our God, our Father, our Daddy like? Based on well-known Bible stories and narrated in the first person by the protagonists, these stories reflect God's character in His intervention in the events of the protagonists. God is love. God is almighty. God is compassionate. God is merciful. God is caring. God is our Father. He is intimately involved in our lives, and we are His children. We call Him Abba, Father, Daddy.

We all find ourselves in the lion's den from time to time. We encounter difficulties, we face circumstances beyond our control or understanding, and we experience the darkness of fear, uncertainty, perplexity, confusion, and doubt. The stories in the *Who's Your Daddy?* Series articulate the fact that we are not alone, that God is with us, that He hears our prayers and responds with love and care to our individual needs and circumstances according to His will and purpose.

They assure us that God is with us—always, in every circumstance—and we should trust Him with childlike faith, reminding us that we are beloved children of God. As I read these stories, again and again, I recalled the words of Paul in Romans 8:38–39:

> For I am convinced that nothing can ever separate us from his love. Death can't, and life can't. The angels won't, and all

> the powers of hell itself cannot keep God's love away. Our fears for today, our worries about tomorrow, or where we are—high above the sky, or in the deepest ocean—nothing will ever be able to separate us from the love of God demonstrated by our Lord Jesus Christ when he died for us. (NLT)

"I knew and trusted God in a way that was childlike;" affirms the protagonist of the story "Dinner for One!" How reassuring are the words of Angel in that story: "Daniel, you need to remember; you're not alone, you know. He not only hears your prayers, Your God responds to them too."

Jennifer Williams
Methodist University Department Chair:
and Associate Professor of Spanish;

Preface

This book is not a collection of Bible stories but rather a collection of Bible-based stories for your reflection. It was born out of a desire to explore and express how individuals in the Scriptures (who were people like you and me, not made-up characters in a play) may have felt and thought as they went through different experiences in their lives.

The general theme is one that is evident and close to my heart: the longing bond between sons and fathers and those who fill those places in our lives as we navigate through different issues and events.

No one can deny that every generation has their own experiences to face. Our grandfathers' lives were different from our fathers' lives, and we in turn have a different view on life based on how we were raised, what we were exposed to, and the general development of the world around us that affects how we speak, think, and understand.

Today, our children are exposed to issues and themes at earlier ages than we were. But there are a few things that remain constant regardless of the changes of time. One is the love, acceptance, and protection a child desires from his or her parents.

Many people may see the Bible as irrelevant to today's society. Some may look at it as the love letter giving account of the unique ways our heavenly Father reached out to humankind.

But I would also like to suggest to those who may have overlooked the notion that the Bible not only teaches us by instruction and example how God relates to us but also how we should relate to each other as people, as families, as children of God.

I believe the previous generation of ministers faithfully taught us the way of salvation, Bible doctrines, church order, and behavior. In this current generation, one can see many of today's ministers (especially the international ones) have taken to task family and relationship issues, using the Bible as a basis for a "whole life salvation," not just the gospel for the soul.

It is with this backdrop in my spirit that I present this first collection. The stories are written in the first person, with the hope you will feel a part of the experience and not just read about a topic.

I hope you enjoy reading it and possibly find things you can relate to. Part 1 begins with a nativity story, followed by part 2, Sons, part 3, Fathers, and ending with part 4, the Easter edition of *Who's Your Daddy? Bible-Based Stories Showing God As A Father for Us All.*

Wherever you are in your journey of self-discovery, it is my hope that you will find the joy and peace you are looking for. I found that a void in my life was filled when I discovered that the heavenly Father is a "father to the fatherless" (Psalm 68:5).

Part 1
A Nativity Story

It is coming down to the last hours before the birth of Jesus. Mary and Joseph are anxiously looking for a place to stay in Bethlehem. Even though the couple have received confirmation from the angel Gabriel that the babe who is conceived in Mary is from the Holy Spirit, the circumstances seem to outweigh the promise.

Balthazar, Casper, and Melchior have read the Scriptures and star alignments and have embarked on a journey to find the child they believe to be the promised Messiah.

A small group of shepherds huddled around a small fire on the hills of Judah, keeping watch over their flock, contemplate, "Is the future of our nation to be ruled by the Roman Empire, or will the word of the Lord in Micah 5:2, which says, 'But you, Bethlehem Ephrathah, though you are small among the clans of Judah, out of you will come for me one who will be ruler over Israel, whose origins are from of old, from ancient times, come to pass?"

As the sequence of events unfolds, caught right in the middle of this miraculous event are the innkeeper and his wife, whose hearts of compassion go far and beyond to help the young couple they find standing at their door.

At one point, things seem hopeless, especially for Joseph, who is used to providing for his family. But each participant in his or her own way learns a most valuable lesson: when all is said and done, the Father is still on the throne, and though weeping may endure through the night, joy comes in the morning.

The Inn

In those days Caesar Augustus issued a decree that a census should be taken of the entire Roman world. (This was the first census that took place while Quirinius was governor of Syria.) and everyone went to their own town to register. *(Luke 2:1–3)*

"This has been one of the toughest days ever." I looked at Eve, who appeared as tired as me.

"Well, Adam, it's not as if we didn't know this day was coming. Since the time the decree was published by Caesar, people have been pouring into Bethlehem."

I looked out one of the windows facing the street. It was like a ghost town. Everyone who didn't have a relative to stay with found lodging in the city inns. Business was good. Our inn was fully occupied. We even had relatives bunking in the same rooms.

"Adam, are you going to look in on the children?"

"Yes, dear. I'll be up in a minute."

I took a last look out on the deserted street, checked to make sure all the doors were locked, and went upstairs.

"Dad?"

"Yes, baby girl?"

"If you weren't an innkeeper, who would you want to be?"

I looked thoughtfully at my daughter Joanna. "Well, honey, I guess if I weren't an innkeeper, I would like to be a king, maybe from the East, with a palace and camels and horses and a thousand dresses just for you."

"Oh, Dad, you're so funny."

We laughed a little, and I tucked her into bed. Then I went to my bedroom and settled in for the night.

"I wonder if anyone else is still coming to town," Eve said.

"Well, if they are, there's no space here. All I can do is wish them good luck finding somewhere to sleep."

"I guess the only place left is the barn," said Eve with a smile.

The Desert

"Well, what do we have here?" I said to my second-in-command. As my entourage came over a sand dune, I recognized the two caravans of travelers. One was traveling from the southeast and the other from the southwest. But my group was traveling westerly.

"Casper, Melchior … greetings, brothers."

"And you, Balthazar," said Casper.

"It's good to see you both," said Melchior, smiling.

Casper was a serious man who never spoke much. Melchior, on the other hand, had a cheerful spirit.

Our caravans met in the middle of the level of sand.

"So we are agreed," I said, "that the prophet Isaiah did say a virgin shall bring forth a child, and his name shall be called Immanuel."

"Yes, and the star has led us all to this point," said Melchior.

"Do you think it might happen tonight?" asked Casper, looking up at the night sky.

"I don't know for sure. But when it happens, we'll know."

"This is a good place to camp for the night," Melchior volunteered.

"Yes, I agree." I called back to the group of men following me. "We'll camp here for tonight." Each of us had eight to ten servants in addition to a handful of colleagues accompanying us for the journey.

The desert was a peaceful place. It was warm, and the night was filled with stars. But there was one star that shone brighter than the rest.

"Is it my imagination, or is the star that led us to this point getting brighter?" asked Casper.

"I wonder …" started Melchior, while gazing up in the night sky. "Could it be that the King of Kings, the Lord of Lords, the Savior of the world is to be born this night? If it is so, we will not be there to welcome him into the world."

"Whether we welcome him at his birth or after, we will find him," I said, the anticipation of the event growing inside me. "Anyway, let's make camp. Then we can share our findings about the coming of the Messiah."

The Journey

So Joseph also went up from the town of Nazareth in Galilee to Judea, to Bethlehem the town of David, because he belonged to the house and line of David. He went there to register with Mary, who was pledged to be married to him and was expecting a child. *(Luke 2:4–5)*

"Mary?"

"Yes, Joseph?"

"How are you doing?"

"I think he's going to be born tonight. We need to find a place to stay. How far are we from Bethlehem?"

"It should be just over this ridge."

As we came over the slope, we saw Bethlehem.

Finally, I said in my heart. Mary and I looked at each other and smiled.

A lot had happened before we had come to this point. I was told not to be afraid by an angel in my dreams regarding taking Mary as my wife. I loved her … no, I *love* her. I always have. But this was something I'd never seen before, not even in the Scriptures. "A virgin will bring forth a son, and his name shall be called Jesus." At first I couldn't handle it. It was blowing my mind. But after the angelic visit, I began to gain control of myself. And now God's Son was about to be born. I only wished I knew where.

"You're very quiet, Joseph."

"I was just thinking about where we're going to stay. We must be the last ones into the city by the looks of it."

"It does look a bit shaky. But just because we don't know where to go doesn't mean God has not provided a place for us. He wouldn't bring us this far to leave us."

Mary smiled as she spoke. She had such faith in God that at times I marveled at how sincere and innocent her spirit was. It was no wonder she was chosen to carry the child. She was a blessing to everyone around her. Granted, it hadn't been easy with people speaking behind our backs, saying, "Why couldn't they have waited until they were married?" But with everything Mary went through, she always knew in her heart that if God had told no one else, he had spoken to her.

"Joseph?"

"Yes, dear?"

"Let's try this place."

We had come to the first inn on the street. We stopped, and I knocked on the door several times. Finally, I heard a latch open, and then a small window in the door about the size of a man's face opened.

"What do you want?" growled the innkeeper.

"Finally! My wife is pregnant and expecting our child a short while from now. Please help us. Do you have a room? We'll take anything you have."

"Mister, I can't believe you came to Bethlehem in her condition. My place is full. Try down the street. But you must know, it looks like everywhere is full."

He looked at Mary and then at me and shut the window. We were about to leave when the latch opened again.

"Listen. I'm sorry. I really don't have any space, but if there's anyone who might be able to help you now, it's Adam. He and his wife, Eve, run the inn at the end of this street. Everywhere is locked up, but as good people go, they are your best bet for finding some place for the night." He looked at Mary and then back at me and nodded.

"Well, Mary, you heard the man. Let's see if Adam and Eve can help us."

The Archangels

"So, Gabriel."

"Yes, Michael?"

"You've been a very busy boy, haven't you?"

We both laughed.

"Michael, what a season it has been. First, there was Zachariah. I had to go to him to tell him his wife, Elizabeth, was going to have a child and that the child was going to be the forerunner for the Son of God."

"And how did that go?"

"You would have thought that the presence of an angel alone would have been enough to convince any man of the Word of the Lord. But who knew? The man didn't believe me. And you know what the Lord said to do?"

"I know, but tell me anyway. I can always do with a good laugh."

"I had to strike the fellow dumb!"

Michael was laughing but trying to hold it by covering his mouth with his hand.

"Yes, yes," said Michael, smiling, "but I understand it gets better."

"Gets better? You're really enjoying this, aren't you?" I said with a smile on my face. "Well …" I continued, "it does get better. Imagine—Joseph is falling apart when he hears that Mary is going to have a child. So I'm supposed to go down and talk with him and tell him everything's going to be all right and not to worry; the baby is not his, it is the Lord's."

"Okay, okay," said Michael.

"But the man is so tense, every time I go down to talk to him, it's like he's having a private earthquake, and I can't get to speak to him at all."

"So what happened?" Michael asked, still smiling.

"I had to wait until Joseph was asleep. Then, when he was finally resting, I got the chance to speak to him in his dreams."

Michael started laughing again. "You've had a difficult time, my friend!"

"Michael, let's put fun and jokes aside for a minute. Do you want to hear something truly, truly wonderful?" Michael settled down to hear what I had to say. "The only person who handled my presence and what I had to say with grace … was Mary."

Michael nodded.

"I tell you, my brother, she was a bit startled by my presence at first, which, given the circumstances, is understandable. But when it came to her assignment, what the Lord was calling her to do"—I shook my head in amazement—"she accepted it willingly and with such grace when she said she was the Lord's servant."

"Well, Gabriel," Michael started, "if anyone had any doubts about the Lord's choice, this can teach us a key thing. Our Lord always chooses the right person for the right job."

"Amen to that."

"So, you have another trip?"

"Yes, it's approaching the time when I find the persons to stand as witnesses to Jesus's birth."

"Has He told you?"

"Yes, it's a group of shepherds in the fields nearby. But I'm going down first to bring the good news, and then a company of angels is going to join me in celebration. Oh, that reminds me—we have one more rehearsal before the main event. See you later, brother— will you be around for the show?"

"I wouldn't miss it for the world," said Michael, smiling.

The Barn

> While they were there, the time came for the baby to be born, and she gave birth to her firstborn, a son. She wrapped him in cloths and placed him in a manger, because there was no guest room available for them. (Luke 2:6–7)

"Okay, Mary, we're here."

We stopped just outside the inn, and I went to knock on the door. I raised my hand to knock and held it in the air.

"Joseph, what's wrong? Are you okay?" Mary asked.

I always had enough money to get the things I needed. I wasn't a wealthy man, but I was okay. I could provide for my family, and in the area where I lived, I was known as the lender, not the borrower. I was one of those people one would come to for help or advice.

But here, right now, standing before the door of this inn and having the fate of my wife's wellbeing dependent on whether the person behind this door said yes or no made me feel vulnerable. Really, really helpless.

"Mary, I'm fine, dear. I'll just be a second."

I needed help, and I needed it now. "Lord, I need You now. Please give us favor. I don't understand why Your Son wasn't born in a palace. Isn't a palace the place where kings are born? But right now this is the best I can do, and my best is not enough."

I could feel the tears running down my face. "If not for my sake, or Mary's, but that You be glorified. Please, Lord, may there be room for us here tonight."

I knocked on the door. No answer. I knocked again and waited. Then a window opened from the floor above.

"Hello, sir," I said, looking up.

"Goodness, man, what are you doing out this time of night?"

"My wife is heavy with child, so our journey has been slow and long."

"Adam, what is it? Who's out there?"

"Go back to bed, Eve—I can handle this."

"I am sorry to trouble you," I said, my voice almost breaking "I really am, but my wife needs a place to rest. We have a child on the way, and the innkeeper down the street said if anyone can help us, it's you. Please, sir, please."

***

I looked down at the man in the street. Having a wife and children of my own, I knew what it was like to be in a vulnerable position. It wasn't about seeking help for me but for my family.

"Hold on, I'm coming down," I called to the man standing at my door.

Eve got out of bed and put on her nightgown. "If you think I'm going to let you go down there by yourself, you have another thing coming, mister."

As a married man I knew when to argue and when not to. This wasn't the time to argue. We lit a lamp and set off down the stairs. The inn was so full we had people sleeping in the lobby area near the fireplace, just to get in out of the cold air.

I opened the door and saw the man had already taken his wife off the donkey, and both were waiting in the doorway.

"Oh my goodness, dear," Eve cried out quietly. "Come in, come in."

I took his bags and set them on the floor, then got the young lady a chair to sit on. "Where are you both coming from?" I asked.

"From Nazareth," the young man answered. "Thank you for opening your door. We're grateful to you both."

"Opening a door is one thing," I replied, "but finding a place to sleep is next to impossible."

"Adam."

"Yes, dear."

"We can't leave them like this—not on God's good earth we can't."

"But what do you want me to do?"

"Think of something; you always do, husband of mine."

I looked at the man, and I could see in his eyes that failure was not an option. Then the young girl started to breathe heavily.

"Oh, Joseph, I think he's coming. Help me, please."

"Eve."

"Yes, dear?"

"Remember that joke we shared earlier about if anyone else came looking for room tonight?" I looked at my wife and shrugged my shoulders.

"Darling, you're a genius. I knew there was a reason I married you," Eve said with a smile. "Come with me, child." Eve helped up the young girl on her left side while the young man supported her on her right.

"Follow me," I said to them.

I led them through the inn and into the kitchen. We went through the store room and out the back door. Crossing over a few feet was a small barn we had to keep a few animals.

"Well, it's not the inn, but it will keep you safe. There's water and hay to keep you warm."

"Thank you," the young man said. "You've been most kind. May the Lord bless you and your household."

"And you."

"Oh, sorry, in all the anticipation to find a place, I forgot to introduce ourselves. My name is Joseph, and this is my wife, Mary."

"I'm Adam, and this lovely lady is my wife, Eve."

"Joseph, I need you."

"I'm coming, Mary."

"Well, we'll leave you to it."

Then Eve gave me a stern look.

"Maybe we'll hang around a bit, just to make sure you're okay," I said, smiling pleasantly.

"Is that okay with you, Ms. Eve?" I said in a patronizing tone.

She just looked at me and smiled. Then I heard her whisper to Mary, "That's my husband, and thank the Lord I got one of the good ones."

Mary smiled.

I stood in the background while Joseph and Eve helped Mary deliver the baby. Then I heard a cry.

"It's a boy," said Eve.

"We knew," said Mary.

I knit up my eyebrows. How on earth could she know whether the child would be a boy or a girl before he was born?

I looked on as Joseph and Eve washed the baby and then wrapped him with some linen cloth we used for milking.

"Let's leave them now," said Eve. "They've had a long trip, and now the baby is safe. They all could do with some rest."

"Well, can I make one suggestion?" I added. "It may not be much, but here, I cleaned it out while I was waiting." I handed Joseph a manger that we used to feed lambs. "You can line the inside with hay and use it to rest the baby."

For a moment I held my breath a bit, wondering if I had made a good suggestion.

"This will do just fine," said Joseph with a smile.

"Oh, good then," I replied.

"Come on, husband," said Eve. "Joseph has everything under control from here."

The Confirmation

After Jesus was born in Bethlehem in Judea, during the time of King Herod, Magi from the east came to Jerusalem. (Matthew 2:1)

"What is it, Balthazar?" asked Melchior.

"The star," I replied. "Look at the star."

"It's glowing brighter," said Casper.

"The King is born," I said. "The Savior of the world is born."

"May God be praised," cried Melchior.

We woke all the men. "The Savior is born," shouted Casper. "Come, let us give thanks and praise, for the Savior of the world has come to set the captive free."

The men started singing and shouting. Some were on their knees bowing continuously with clasped hands. It was a joyous occasion.

"Tell me, Balthazar," Melchior said, "how did you know? I know we saw the star, but something tells me you knew something before we did! Did you have a dream? A vision? Humor me, my friend. How did you know this was the time?"

I breathed in deeply and let out the air. I looked at Melchior intently and wondered if he would even believe me.

"Balthazar, we are all here by faith in the Holy Scriptures. If one believes in faith, then I doubt there is very little else left to believe."

"You have a point there, Melchior." By this time Casper had rejoined us near the fire.

"How can I put this?" I started out. "Have you ever had a situation where your wife was soon to deliver her child, but you could not be there to see it?"

Melchior and Casper looked at me intently.

"Well, last year while studying at the library, my wife was soon to deliver our child. The servants ran back to me, urging me to leave my studies and be near her. I kept putting them off, telling them that usually she would spend days in labor and that this time was no different."

"So what happened?" asked Casper.

"After a while I grew tired of studying—and their pestering—so I decided to head home. But the strangest thing happened."

Casper and Melchior looked at each other and then turned their attention back to me.

"I was walking back to the main house and looked up at the night sky, and then it hit me."

"What hit you?" asked Melchior.

"It was like a moving in my spirit, and I knew my child was born. Even though I was between the library and the main house, I could feel something that told me he had entered the world."

"Interesting," said Melchior

"Very,", added Casper.

"And this moving in your spirit," continued Melchior, "you felt it again, just a while ago?"

"It was as if something witnessed in my spirit that the Son of God was born." I smiled.

The Fields

And there were shepherds living out in the fields nearby, keeping watch over their flocks at night. (Luke 2:8)

"Can anyone tell me why I took this job in the first place?" I really believed taking care of sheep was a daytime job, but believe me, the nights were getting cold.

"David, did anyone ever tell you that you talk too much?" asked Jesse.

"Yes, his mother," Solomon said, laughing.

The three of us were on the night shift. I got this job through family connections as we were all related. It was a common thing for brothers and cousins to work in the family business together, like fishermen, farmers, and cattle herders.

"The sheep have been good tonight," said Solomon.

"Yes, it has been quiet," commented Jesse. "None have gone wondering off, and we've had no attacks."

Things could go from calm to chaos very quickly working out in the fields, but it was more quiet and peaceful most nights. The night sky looked like a blanket with stars. There wasn't a cloud in sight.

"David."

"Yes, Jesse?"

"When we keep the night watch over the sheep does anything come to mind?"

"What, you mean besides the comfort of a warm bed?" said Solomon jokingly.

I thought about Jesse's question. What part of looking after sheep had to do with life?

"Well, I know my namesake penned the twenty-third Psalm while tending sheep. And he pictured the way our God took care of him," I answered.

"And He will take care of all who trust Him." said Solomon.

"But it's like a dark cloud has set over the people for so long now. With the Romans and the taxes, not to mention when we even go to the synagogue to worship, I feel more reminded of how lost I feel than of hope I have for the future."

Jesse and Solomon looked at me with smiles that said, "I know how you feel."

"I don't believe our God has left us," said Jesse. "Does the sun rise each day?"

"Yes, it does," I answered

"Then who knows the day when the Lord will come to our rescue?"

The Message

An angel of the Lord appeared to them, and the glory of the Lord shone around them, and they were terrified. (Luke 2:9)

Then I noticed something I didn't see before.

"Look over there," I said, pointing to Bethlehem. "That star is really bright."

"Yes, and it seems so low to earth," added Solomon.

"As if it's pointing to somewhere." said Jesse.

Boom.

There was a bright light that lit up the hilltop. It pushed the darkness away and shone all around us.

I covered my face so I would not be blinded from it. When my eyes started to adjust to the light, I found myself squinting them in an effort to see where the light was coming from.

And then I saw him.

He was floating in the air looking down at us. His clothes and face shone. I had never seen anything so beautiful.

He told us not to fear and the news he brought was wonderful for the entire world. The Son of God, the Savior of the world, was born in the city of David. He told us we would find Him in a manger, wrapped in linen cloth.

Then the heavens seemed to burst with light. At one point I thought the starts had turned into angels as they joined him in singing the most beautiful song:

"Glory to God in the highest heaven,
and on earth peace to those on whom his favor rests."

Then as suddenly as they came, they were gone.

"Do you believe what just happened?" asked Solomon.

"I do," I stammered. "I've never seen anything like it."

I was still trying to catch my breath.

"We need to go," ordered Jesse.

"What ... go?" stuttered Solomon.

We were still trying to get our heads around it, but Jesse was ready.

"Didn't you just hear what the angel said?" he said excitedly. "This is what we have been waiting for, for so long. Are you really going to miss this opportunity to witness the birth of the Savior?"

"But wouldn't a King be born in a palace or a royal home? The angel said we will find Him in a manger," I said, still feeling a bit apprehensive. Then Jesse said something that removed all doubt.

"To part the Red Sea, He used a staff; to slay Goliath, He used a stone; and to stop the sun from going down, He used raised hands. My brothers, how many times did our God come to the rescue of His people with less and did so much more? Let us not be like the children of old, who every time our God did a wonderful thing, they cast doubt on His goodness. Tonight we have been favored by Jehovah."

"Yes, you're right, Jesse," answered Solomon. "We need to go to Bethlehem to see this thing the Lord has blessed us of all people to see."

"Then, brethren," I added, "let's not delay any longer—and I think I know just the place to look for Him."

I pointed to the star that was shining as bright as ever. We looked at each other and smiled.

"Let's go."

Who's Your Daddy?

And they came with haste, and found Mary, and Joseph, and the babe lying in a manger. (Luke 2:16)

Mary was resting, and the baby was making little cooing sounds beside her. "Joseph?"

"Yes, my love?"

"Aren't you going to sleep? We can all rest now."

"Soon, dear, soon; I'm just so happy and relieved. It's hard to try and sleep now." I smiled.

I went over to the barn window and looked up at the night sky.

"Lord, thank You for your provision and for carrying us through. Lord, there were moments I was afraid. It wasn't so much for me but for Mary and the child. If anything happened to them, I don't know what I would do. But thank You, Lord, for making a way when I saw no way."

Then as I looked up in the night sky, I saw the brightest star I had ever seen, and it seemed to shine right over the barn. I smiled, and just when I was thinking to myself how nice it looked, I heard voices at the barn door.

"This must be the place."

"Look at the star—it's pointing us right here."

There was a light knock on the door, and I went over to answer it. "Yes?" I said, wondering who else would be around this time of night.

"Hello, I'm Jesse, and these are my brethren, Solomon and David. Is this where the Son of God is born?"

I smiled, and my heart felt like it was beating with joy.

"The Son of God," I repeated. "Yes, come in, come in, but please be quiet … Mother and child are resting."

"We are shepherds," said Jesse. "We were in the fields watching over our sheep when an angel visited us and gave us the good news. Does that sound strange to you?"

"My brother, after what we've gone through, that sounds just … about … right."

And then from the throne room of glory,
to the cradle on earth,
the heavenly Father spoke to His newborn Son.
"My boy, my beautiful, beautiful boy …

Part 2
Sons

Have you ever been scared for your life like a young boy named Daniel when faced with fighting a giant of a man?

Have you ever been let down by someone you looked up to, only to find the person who came through for you was the least likely one to do so?

Have you ever thought, *How could God ever use a person like me to make a miracle happen and touch thousands of lives?*

These stories are about people like you and me and how they managed to get through difficult situations. First Timothy 4:12 says, "Don't let anyone look down on you because you are young, but set an example for the believers in speech, in conduct, in love, in faith and in purity."

These boys and young men found new faith, hope, and love as they went through their experiences. As you read their stories, it is my hope that you will see how they were able to answer one simple question:

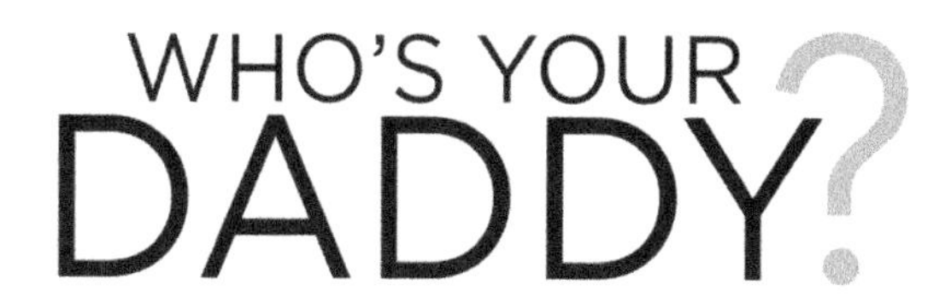

A Boy Set Free

David and his men reached Ziklag on the third day. Now the Amalekites had raided the Negev and Ziklag. They had attacked Ziklag and burned it, and had taken captive the women and everyone else in it, both young and old. They killed none of them, but carried them off as they went on their way. (1 Samuel 30:1–2)

My feet and knees were bleeding from the walk. The army that took us came when Dad and his friends were away. We had been walking for a few days now, stopping occasionally for water and a rest. After a few days' journey, we reached a city. As I looked through the fence they built to hold us, I could see them laughing and drinking, celebrating their "victory."

When they took us, they only found the mothers and children. We had no protection, no soldiers, no one. Dad told me he and his friends would be gone for only a few days, and when he got back we would have time together. He promised. Why was this happening?

At first I felt betrayed, then scared, and then I felt a darkness and anger start to fill me inside.

"Daniel," my mother said, "don't worry; your father will come for us soon." She looked down at me and smiled.

My mother was a very beautiful lady. She was kind and thoughtful. Her name was Abigail, and she loved and respected my dad; anyone could see that by the way they were together. Sometimes I would catch them looking at each other, smiling, even when Dad was in a meeting with the elders of the tribe.

I wasn't a troublesome boy, but I didn't like being played with, and because of that, some of Dad's friends thought I was too old for my age.

Slap … I felt the blow strong and hard on my face.

"Get away from the fence, boy, before I have to clap you again."

The soldier's voice was rough and growling. My mother came up and grabbed me from behind, putting her arms around me and pulling me away from the fence.

"Leave him alone. He's done nothing wrong," she shouted.

"Keep him away from the fence." He took a step toward her.

I broke her grasp and took a step toward him, looking up at his face and staring him in the eye.

"Stop playing around," another soldier shouted. "After all, it looks like the boy would be too much a match for you."

Laughter came from a group of men standing nearby, and then the soldier said, "Mark my words, boy—I'll deal with you soon enough."

"My father is going to kick your ... hup." My mother covered my mouth with her hand before I could finish.

"Daniel," she whispered, "now is not the time."

"You better keep a leash on your boy if you want him to live to see tomorrow," the soldier said angrily.

"Oh, I'm sure he will outlive both of us," replied my mother in a very precise, direct tone, looking at him unnerved. He turned and headed back to his friends.

She bent down and held my face with both hands. "Daniel, you must try and keep that temper of yours. I don't know what I would do if anything happened to you."

"Yes, Mother. I'm sorry."

I usually sat down near the wooden fence anyway. Holding on to it with both hands, I looked at the men who had taken us captive as they walked by casually, talking and laughing as they went.

I could remember how I used to feel, carefree with my brothers and sisters playing in the fields near what used to be our camp, now just a collection of burned-down tents and huts—the place we called home.

Father had left a few days before we were attacked. He promised us that when he came back, he would bring fine linen, gold, cattle, and sheep. Father usually kept his promises.

What happened now? Where was his army? Had they forgotten us? Were they attacked and killed before we were captured? All these questions kept running through my mind, and then I asked myself, "Did my dad ever love me in the first place?"

My thoughts were shaken by loud shouting by the guards. Soldiers were running backward and forward, as if they were confused.

"What's going on?" I heard a soldier ask nervously.

"It's David," another shouted. "David's army is coming."

David's army is coming—the words rang in my heart. Dad's coming. My father is coming. At that moment a feeling of peace and relief swept over me, followed by guilt and shame.

My father was fighting to save us. My mother told me not to lose heart, but there I was, thinking my dad didn't want me. I felt like I had let him down. The noise grew louder and louder. The sound of fighting increased as it got nearer to us.

And then I felt a large hand grab the back of my shirt, pick me up, and throw me into a clearing. I landed on my back and felt my right shoulder bang with pain as it took the brunt of the fall.

"I told you, boy, that you wouldn't live long." It was the soldier I had stood up to. "If I can't kill David then I guess his son will have to do."

His sword was drawn, and there was a big grin on his face as he walked toward me. Using my feet, I began to push myself backward, wriggling my back as I tried to get away.

My heart began to race. I wanted to cry out for help, but nothing would come from my throat. And then, as if he was right there beside me, I heard my father's voice.

"Daniel, remember the story of how I killed a lion when I was just a bit older than you?"

Then the story I heard so many times came back to me. My dad told us of a time when he used to tend sheep. When he was a lad, he was attacked by a lion. As a shepherd, the two things he carried as weapons were a sling and a staff.

When the lion came to take a sheep, he held his staff with both hands, pointing it to him. Not teasing, he kept his eye on it and then knelt down, slowly laying the staff low to the ground. Then, when the lion pounced on him, he lifted the staff with the end set firmly in the ground for support and aimed the top of the staff into the lion's mouth.

He told us how he felt the breath of the lion as it fell into his staff. "Always keep your nerve," he would tell us. "There's nothing wrong with being afraid, but when you keep your nerve, you will know how to act."

I slowed my breathing and tried to focus. What was around me that I could use to defend myself? The soldier was coming closer. Just then I felt soft sand beneath my hands.

I grabbed a handful and stopped kicking. The sand was making it difficult to move, and I wanted to reserve my strength.

"I've got you now, boy," he said, grinning, and raised his sword above his head.

"Not today," I shouted and threw the sand straight into his face. It blinded his eyes, and I threw some more. He started swinging wildly; I dodged each strike as his sword hit the ground.

***

We came on horseback to the top of the ridge overlooking the camp. Joab had taken most of the men and attacked the site. As I looked over the fighting, I could see the women and children behind the fences. What was their prison had become their protection. Then I saw him; my son, my boy.

"My lord. Daniel."

"I know—I see him."

At first my heart froze. My boy was on his back fighting a giant of a man with nothing but a handful of sand. Now where had I seen this before? I smiled and turned to my guard.

"Bow."

"Yes, my lord."

"Arrow."

The small group of men with me were silent but eager to join the fray.

"Steady, boy, steady." Even my horse was anxious to get down to the battle.

I pulled back the arrow on the string, raising the bow through the line of soldiers fighting. The man's arm was raised, as if to land a final blow, and then I saw it—a gap, right in the shoulder blade.

Twang.

***

I prepared myself to shift, then, *thud.* The soldier held his right shoulder and gave out a shout of pain, "Arrrrrr." When he turned, I could see an arrow sticking out of his back.

"Leave him and come on," another soldier shouted. "It's not worth it; if we stay any longer then we all die." The soldier grabbed his wounded friend and both took off, running into the dusty wind. When they left, I sighed with relief. I felt so tired and drained. There was no energy left for me to stand. My eyes closed as I fell into darkness.

I awoke to the sounds of friends and family being united. There was crying and laughing. Children and women were finding their fathers, husbands, brothers, and friends.

"He's awake." It was the voice of my mother. "We were worried about you. Are you okay?" I looked at her, gave a little smile, and nodded my head. "My little soldier," she said. "I'm so proud of you."

With her help I was able to get up and stand on my feet. Then, looking up I saw him. My dad was surrounded by my relatives and friends. "Come on, Daniel," my brother called out. "Dad's here, he's here." I tried to look at him, but I couldn't raise my head. I wanted to, but I squeezed my eyes closed tight, fighting back the tears. I felt so ashamed that I couldn't go to him.

"Daniel," my father, said walking toward me. "What's wrong, boy?"

I could sense the concern in his voice. "I thought you weren't coming back." My eyes were closed; I still couldn't get myself to look at him. "I haven't been a good son. I'm sorry, Father. I'm sorry."

Then Dad got down on one knee, and I felt his hand on my shoulder. "Daniel, listen to me. I love you, I love all my family, but the thing is, of all the children, I knew you could take care of yourself and your mother."

I raised my head and looked at him with a relaxed smile. "I'm so proud of you, and I came back for all my family. After all, whose arrow do you think hit that soldier in his back?"

I gasped, my mouth open. "You saw me?"

"Of course I did, and from a distance I could see all you boys. But you were the only one fighting a soldier. In fact, you kind of reminded me … of me."

Then Dad said with a smile, "I didn't save you from that Goliath. I saved him from you."

"Oh Dad." I threw my arms around his neck, buried my head on his shoulder, and held him tight.

"After all," he said,

A Guide for a Blind Man

> Samson said to the servant who held his hand "Put me where I can feel the pillars that support the temple, so that I may lean against them." (Judges 16:26)

My father was a kind, elderly man. He was thin and bald. He wasn't a muscular or tall person like some of my friends' fathers were, but when it came to the synagogue, he was there every Sabbath. He disciplined himself to say prayers and to give an offering from what he made selling doves and pigeons from his stall.

We lived near the Coliseum, where I would spend time working for the guards. My duties involved bringing food for the prisoners and water from the well outside, plus any other odd jobs they wanted me to do.

There was one prisoner I felt sorry for every time I saw him. I couldn't understand how he ended up like this if he was the same man my father spoke of almost every night.

"Samson is a judge of Israel," my father would say. "He did many great things in the strength of Jehovah." Then he would recount the stories of how he slew an army of Philistines with just the jawbone of a donkey or the time when he tied foxes together, lit their tails on fire, and set them free to run in the fields of the enemies of Israel, destroying their crops.

He made him sound as if he was a superhero by the way he described Samson's battles and the way he played tricks on his enemies. But when Father told these stories, I couldn't help but wonder, why couldn't he be more like Samson?

Often in the marketplace I could hear my friends' fathers talking with him. "Why do you sell your goods at such low prices? Visitors to the city need doves to make sacrifices in the temple, and instead of raising the prices to catch them, you keep them at the same price for everyone. Come on, man, you're missing out on making a healthy profit."

Then, they would laugh at him in a way that wasn't exactly insulting but more of a shared joke. He called them his friends and didn't take them seriously. He always believed that if people came to worship Jehovah, he didn't want to use their need to offer a sacrifice as a means to make a profit. I didn't understand it, but that was my dad.

"Come here, boy," a soldier called to me. "Go get some water from the well; we have a prisoner who needs cleaning up." I picked up my bucket and ran through the corridors of the prison.

Over time I became very familiar with the corridors that led in and out of the prison cells below the Coliseum. I didn't like working there much. I saw a lot of misery, but it was the only place I could find work apart from with my father, who I felt embarrassed to be with. Once in a while I would find a silver coin dropped by a guard or trader as they did business within the prison walls.

"What's happening?" I heard a guard ask as he came into the main holding area to start duty.

"Oh, it seems the delegates are having a big party in the Coliseum. They're coming from all over the city for some sort of celebration."

"Hey, you there—yes, you, boy."

"Yes sir," I answered.

"Take this letter down to cell 3B, and give it to the guard at the front."

I took the letter and headed down the corridor. *3B, 3B, 3B.* Whenever I got an order like that, I tried to remember who the prisoner inside the cell was. This cell I knew without trying; it was Samson's.

"Well what do we have here," the prison guard said as I handed him the letter. "So the blind man is to be released so he can entertain our guests. Well, he might as well; he's just a waste of space down here, and we can use the cell for real criminals." The guards laughed and went back to the main area of level 3.

I stood at the cell door looking at him. My idol, my hero; he looked like a shell of a man. He hadn't eaten for some time. They fed him on scraps. His hair was long, black, and dirty. His clothes were ragged and torn. His head twitched to catch the sounds around him. His ears were his eyes. It was how he saw the world now.

"Who is it? Who's there?"

"It's me, sir."

"Yes, boy, I recognize your voice. What is going on?" Samson asked.

"There's a big party going on upstairs, and people are coming from all over the city. And …"—I stopped and let out a sigh—"they want you to entertain them," I said, hanging down my head in shame.

Wasn't there anyone I could look up to? My hero was in a prison cell, and my Father was a prisoner of his own thinking. Why did my dad have to be so different from everyone else, standing up for what, righteousness?

Look what righteousness got Samson—eyes burned, imprisoned, and humiliated. And as for my dad, he was laughed at behind his back.

The head guard came back. "All right, how am I going to do this? I can't spare a guard just to walk this blind man up to the Coliseum. It's not like he can run and go anywhere. Boy, you know the way up to the main entrance, don't you?"

"Err … yes sir."

"Open the door," he commanded a soldier. The keys clanged on the iron frame. "Take him up to the main entrance of the arena," he told me. And then he threw a silver coin at me, and I caught it by clutching it to my chest.

Samson was chained by his hands to a wall. A guard went in, unchained him, and pulled him out of the cell. As he came to the doorway, the guard let him go, and he fell to the ground.

"I'm not wasting a guard's time just to carry him out. Boy, help him up and make sure you reach the main entrance."

"Yes sir," I replied.

The guards left us, and I bent down to help up Samson. "Boy," he said in the whisper of a voice.

"I'm here, Samson." Tears started to fill my eyes, but I didn't want to make a sound. It was bad enough to see my idol like this and then on top of it, disclose how wretched I felt to see him in this state.

"Give me your hand, boy." I held on to his left arm and braced him as he placed his right hand on the wall to push himself up.

As he stood, he took a deep breath. He looked so tired and broken. It reminded me of when the old lions outlived their usefulness to the guards. They kept them locked up and unfed until there was no more fight in them. At that stage the lions couldn't even let out a roar. Their eyes were droopy, skin saggy; they looked like if you hit them just once, they would fall to the ground. No fight left.

Slowly we made our way through the corridors. It seemed to take forever. "Samson," I started to ask in a trembling voice, "my father says you are a judge of Israel. Then how did you end up here?"

"What does your father do?"

"He sells doves to people who come to worship at the temple."

"Would you say he is an honorable man?"

I paused to think about that question as we passed some more guards sitting around a table. They didn't even bother to give us a second glance.

"I don't know. I haven't thought about that before." I told him how ashamed I felt of my father and how the other men in the area treated him. Samson was silent, as if he was pondering what I said. He didn't speak again until we reached the entrance of the Coliseum.

The daylight was blinding me as we stepped out into the open. It was obvious Samson couldn't see it, but he could feel the sun shining on him, and for a moment, I could see a sense of peace come over his face. The seats were full. People were laughing and drinking. Two small men were play acting a fighting scene in the middle of the courtyard. One was dressed as a soldier and the other in a pig costume.

"Ladies and gentlemen, I present to you the pride of the Israelite people—the great and mighty Samson," the announcer called out from a balcony, pointing at Samson and waving to the crowd. The people laughed and cheered.

"Boy."

"Yes, sir."

"Describe the Coliseum. How is it set up?"

"Well, Samson, there are sixteen pillars that hold the balconies. The pillars are set in a circular structure, eight on each side. Then the whole building is mainly supported by these two larger pillars at this end of the Coliseum. They support the main balcony, which holds the city leaders.

"Guide me to the main pillars."

"Yes, sir."

By this time the people were throwing their leftover food at Samson, drinking and laughing at him. I felt powerless to do anything.

When we got to the pillars, he said, "Young man, listen to me. I am here because of my disobedient heart. I was too weak to control my desires. I asked you if your father was an honorable man. Does he serve the Lord our God?"

"Yes, sir," I replied.

"Does he cheat any man in his dealings?"

"No, sir."

"Does he live to the best of his ability to follow the commandments of the Lord?"

"Sir, I believe he does."

"Then he is a stronger man than I am."

I looked up at him and couldn't believe my ears.

"Strength—true strength—isn't the measure of how much power you yield; it's the courage to stand up and live for God while others around you don't. Remember that, will you?"

"Yes sir, I will."

"Now go. Go and find your father because this place will be no more after today." Then I heard Samson pray, "Lord, in Your grace and mercy, give me strength one more time, and let me die with my enemies."

He began to push against the pillars, but nothing happened. The people kept on laughing. And then, I heard a crack in the ceiling. Dust started to fall from the top of the pillars. There was a sharp rumble, and I saw the facial expressions of the people start to change.

Everyone started to quiet down, and their gaze was fixed on Samson as he continued to push against the pillars. "I think, my boy … it's time for you to leave. Go, join your father, and no matter what happens … don't … turn … back."

I started to back away from Samson. The rumbling got louder and louder. I turned and started to run through the corridors, passing soldiers on my way who were rushing toward the courtyard. Behind me the ceiling started to cave in. I kept running, not daring to look back but made sure I was heading to the nearest exit.

I could hear the shouts and screams of people coming from within the courtyard. "Don't turn back … no matter what … don't turn back." The words echoed in my head.

Suddenly I burst into sunlight, but I kept on running. I could hear the entire structure coming down, bricks and stone falling on top of each other.

"Don't turn back." And I didn't.

I didn't stop until I saw my father in the street.

"Father," I cried.

"Son, I was so worried. I saw the Coliseum falling and prayed to God you were safe."

I ran into his arms and held him tight. "I'm sorry, Father. I am so sorry."

"For goodness' sake, boy, whatever have you done to be sorry for?" I looked up at him and smiled.

"Father."

"Yes, my boy?"

"Do you think I can stay with you at the stall tomorrow?"

"Of course you can, son. After all …

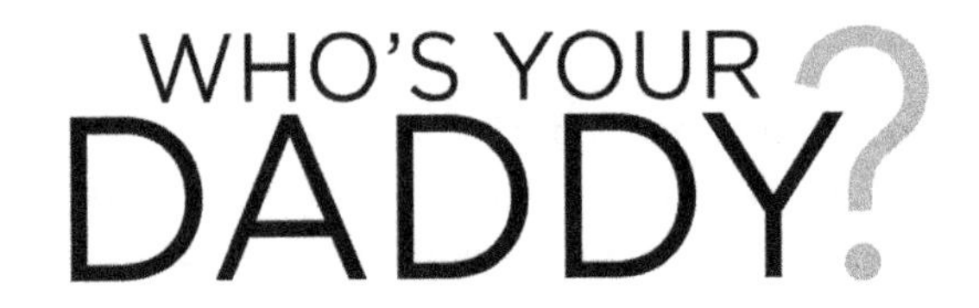

Chosen with Oil

> So Samuel took the horn of oil and anointed him in the presence of his brothers, and from that day on the Spirit of the LORD came powerfully upon David. Samuel then went to Ramah. (1 Samuel 16:13)

Psalm 23 is woven into the story as David speaks his thoughts through his experiences.

"I wonder if this is how being adopted feels. Does being adopted have a different feeling from being born in the family you're raised in? I'm in a family, a big one, but I don't feel like I belong; I feel as if I was switched at birth or my mother could be my mother but I have a different father."

"I wonder if anyone can understand how I feel. When my father looks at my brothers, I can see the pride in his eyes. Yes, they are the next generation of tall, dark, and handsome. But me, it's as if I didn't exist most times. I feel more like a servant or a helper than a son. Like I was a last-minute extension, as if . . ."

Gruuuuuuuu.

"I know that sound"—*bear.*

"Oh God, where are the others. I got so lost in my thoughts that I led the sheep way out in the fields. The grass is so tall here; I can barely see them behind me. I'm looking around, but I can't see another shepherd anywhere."

Gruuuuuuuu.

"Oh boy, there it is again. What to do? What to do? What to do? Okay, now I see him, at least his back anyway, swaying from side to side just above the grass. I didn't realize this grass was so tall. It's at my waist."

"Well, he's about fifty feet away. What is he doing? He's stopped. Now he's lifting his head; he must be smelling the air to pick up the scent of the sheep. Clever."

"Okay, David, keep calm and take a deep breath. How am I going to handle this? There isn't an instruction manual on how to deal with a bear so"—*run*.

"Look at those sheep. I can't leave them like this; they'd be clueless as to what to do. Think, boy, think. Okay … he's running … and right at me … move."

Roarrrr.

His sound was loud, and the sheep darted away in different directions, jumping over each other. "Baa, baa."

They sounded frightened; they could sense the danger.

"Come on, David, they're not the only one with legs. What are you doing? Move, man, move."

I started running back through the field. This bear was fast, and he was gaining on me quick. Running and jumping over tall patches of grass, I spotted an oak tree. The trunk looked a couple of feet wide, more than enough to cover my body if I stood behind it.

"Oh Lord, I need You. There is no one else to call on. Please, Lord, help me. Hear my cry." I ran to the tree, got around it, and crouched down, holding my staff so tight I think my fingerprints started to indent the wood.

"Stand up."

I looked around, but there was no one in sight.

"Stand up."

Pressing my back against the tree, I stood up. The bear was on the other side of the tree, sniffing the ground. I turned around to face the tree and took a step back.

"Ouch," I said.

My right leg scratched against a bush.

"*Roarrrr*," the bear let out and then stood on his hind legs. He balanced himself, waving his arms.

"Wait for it," said that voice again. "Wait."

The bear grabbed at me with both arms by wrapping them around the tree, trying to reach me with his claws. "Now," said the voice.

I jumped on to the tree trunk; with my staff in my right hand, I curved my arm around the tree so my hand would land behind the bear's neck. Then I caught the middle section of the staff with my left hand and braced my feet against the tree.

My knees were almost touching my chest in a squat-like position; I pulled on the staff, which had landed right in the crease of the back of the bear's neck, and pushed with my feet against the tree.

My brothers used to say I was strong and ruddy for my age, like I was built to work on a farm. Right now, that was no solace. "God, please don't make my staff break. This bear's neck has got to go before it does. Anyway, Lord, I don't intend to die today. Please give me the strength."

I pulled on the staff, and my arms and shoulders strained as the bear kept on growling. My eyes pressed closed tight, and sweat was pouring from my brow down my face and neck. *Crack.* I kept on pulling, but there was no resistance. I opened my eyes and looked at the bear; he wasn't moving. I eased my grip and then released my left hand from the staff.

Pushing off from the tree, I landed on my feet. The bear was still holding the tree but motionless. I poked him with my staff, but there was no movement.

Then slowly his arms started to slip off from the tree, and he fell backward to the ground. *Wump.* The sound gave me a sense of relief. I could breathe again. I began to walk backward away from the tree. I didn't feel like exploring any further. One bear was enough; I wasn't going to put myself into the position to run into another.

"Thank You, Lord," I said with a deep sigh. I looked up, and a sense of peace and rest came over me. I was physically tired but had a calm assurance that things were going to be okay.

"David, where have you been? It doesn't matter. Stop playing around. Your Father wants you back at the main house."

"O, hi, Jacob, what's going on?"

"I'm not sure, but all your brothers have come in to see your father, and I think the prophet Samuel is there too."

"So then, I'm the last one he called?"

"Don't take it like that."

"How else should I take it?"

"Well, so what happened to you? Where have you been?"

"I … it doesn't matter. Let's go. Father and the others are waiting."

Jacob was okay. He was one of my father's workers who managed the farm. But it just didn't feel like it would make any sense to recount what I had just gone through. Most probably, they wouldn't believe me anyway.

But that voice—I just couldn't get it out of my mind.

I looked around, and the sheep were still following me. Then the words of a tune I thought about the other day came back to me.

"The Lord is my shepherd, I lack nothing." He leads me as I led the sheep.

"He makes me lie down in green pastures." The peace I feel at times is like the sheep resting with not a care in the world.

"He leads me beside quiet waters, he refreshes my soul." His presence is almost like when I drink water from the brook and feel it refreshing my body and giving me a feeling of new life.

"He guides me along the right paths for his name's sake." No matter what my family may think of me, I will follow the Lord and try my best to do what's right. I go through what I go through for His glory.

"Even though I walk through the darkest valley; I will fear no evil." I never realized caring for sheep would be such a dangerous job. First the lion and now this bear, and there's wolves. But so long as the Lord is with me, I have nothing to fear.

"For you are with me; your rod and your staff, they comfort me." Even as I used my staff to protect the sheep, I believe, "Lord, Your defenses are impossible to penetrate."

"David, wake up, boy. What are you doing, daydreaming?"

Oh no, not again. Lost in a chain of thought. Luckily it wasn't a bear I faced; it was the whole family.

"Come on, boy, stop playing around," my father shouted. The bear was beginning to feel like a better option right now.

My brothers were all lined up like a small army outside the house beside the cattle fence. It was automatic. I joined the end of the line; no one had to tell me where to stand. Then I saw an old man standing beside my Father. I recognized him from the temple, but I'd never met him up close.

"The Lord has spoken. This is the one."

Samuel spoke with such authority and determination. No one dared argue with him. Then he came over to me and in a softer, kinder tone said, "Man may look at the outward appearance, but God, our God, looks at the heart." Then straightening his back, his authoritative voice came back. "Bow on one knee, boy." I obeyed.

He took out a bull's horn from under his coat and raising it above me, began to pour olive oil on my head. I'm not sure what it meant, but as the oil kept pouring through my hair, down my face and ears, on my shoulders, neck, and back, I could sense the possibilities of a bright future.

I knew I wasn't to die that day. The Lord had something great for me to do. I didn't know what it was, but there was something, and until I fulfilled my purpose, I would continue to praise Him for His goodness and mercy.

When I stood up, I could feel the resentment in the air. The way my father looked at me was a look I would never forget. I wonder if he felt I had taken something away from one of my older brothers, as if I didn't deserve to be recognized by the prophet.

When I looked at my brothers, not one of them was happy for me. No one showed any form of gratitude to Samuel that the Lord had chosen someone from our family to represent Him in His service one day. It was very tense.

That night around the dinner table, there wasn't the usual chatter I was accustomed to. Everyone was silent, reflecting on what had just happened. I ate slowly, glancing up from my plate from time to time.

Everyone sitting on each side of the table was just looking at each other. My father was deadly silent. I felt as if at any moment someone was going to throw a knife to try and kill me.

"You prepare a table before me in the presence of my enemies." The thought just burst into my head. "Lord, whoever would believe that I would really have to consider my own family as enemies? I thought enemies were those outside the family home, not inside. Aren't I supposed to feel safe inside, with familiar people and familiar faces?"

But I didn't.

"You anoint my head with oil; my cup overflows." What a day it had been—facing a bear, defending my life and the sheep, and being anointed by the prophet Samuel. And that voice; "Lord, was that You? If so, speak to me please, Lord. I'm sitting at the table, but I've never felt more afraid …"

"Surely your goodness and love will follow me all the days of my life, and I will dwell in the house of the Lord forever."

"Okay, Lord, I'm beginning to get it. When my mother and father forsake me, You will take me up. What do You say to that, Lord?"

Then the voice I heard before whispered in my heart:

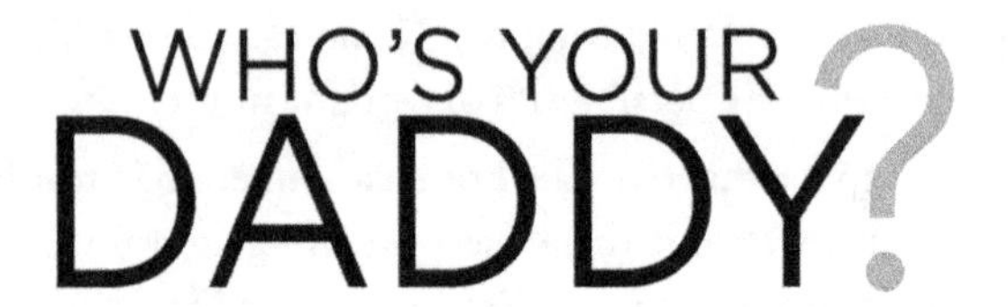

How Did I End up Like This?

When he came to his senses, he said, "How many of my father's hired servants have food to spare, and here I am starving to death!" (Luke 15:17)

"Get away from me, you filthy animal." If anyone told me pigs could smell this bad, I wouldn't have believed them. My feet were covered in muck, and the squishy feeling of mud and rotten vegetables between my toes made my spine shiver. No human being should be working in these kinds of conditions, let alone living in them. If I had the right frame of mind, I would put in a formal complaint to the manager. Yeah, like that would make a difference.

You know another embarrassing thing about this situation? You see, if you're not used to nice things, don't get me wrong—it's not a proud thing or a, "I'm too special for this job"; it's just that, if your normal everyday clothes are rags, then no one would take a second look or think less of you if they saw you feeding pigs, as this is the lowest job a guy could get.

Do you see what I'm saying here? When you have on your nice, good, fine-printed clothes that are torn and weather beaten, the linings are ripped, and you're covered in dirt and other solutions too degrading to mention … well, people passing by can make the easy assumption that this young lad is not from around here; that for how I was raised, I should not be in this position.

Either I was ambushed, robbed, and have no family or home to return to or I was so stupid with my wealth that I lost everything to drink, gambling, and women. What can I say; I'm guilty of being stupid.

You know what's hurting me now? It's how I spoke to Dad and the guilt trip I laid on him to convince him to give me what I wanted. What made me do it? I'm not sure. Maybe it was the traders who stopped by our home and did business with us. They told us of their travels and the "interesting" things they got up to in the city. I was smitten.

My dad was an older man in his seventies. He had a long white beard and was always smiling. He had a big pot belly, and I liked to play boxing with it. That always made him laugh. And for some unknown reason, he loved the color white. White walls, white drapes, white curtains, white linen, white clothing. Well, you get the picture.

Everyone in the house loved my dad. He had a kind and warm spirit. My mother died when I was younger. I was about eight or nine when she got sick and passed away. She was beautiful, and they loved each other a lot.

After her passing, Dad was sad for a while; I remember how grateful he was to have her in his life. People from all over came to pay tribute to her but mainly because of how he had lived his life. They respected him so much.

I remember one friend of his; they had known each other for over fifty years. At the evening dinner after the funeral, I was standing beside him at a fruit table.

"My boy, I'm sorry for your loss."

"Thank you, sir."

"I know it's a difficult time, but I want you to think about something." I looked up at him, wondering what he was going to say. "Look around you. What do you see?"

"Well, there's my father and my older brother. The servants, my friends, and a lot of people who knew my father and mother."

"Do you know the reason why these people came here today?"

"I think so … to say good-bye to Mom."

"Yes, you're right, but there's something I want you to remember. Your father is a good man. There are not many around like him who are as generous, helpful, and kind and a gentleman."

"What's a gentleman, sir?" I asked with a quizzical look on my face.

"A gentleman is a man who tries to make people around him feel as comfortable as possible. It doesn't matter how near or far they live, what position they have in society, or even if they are wealthy or not."

I looked around the room. Most of these people I had never seen before. And the servants— some were crying, others were moving around, serving and doing their duties in silence.

My father didn't deserve to be so unhappy. After a while he came back to himself again. My mother's presence was greatly missed as she was the lady of the house and the glue that held us all together. We had a large painting made in the main hall in honor of her memory. Every time Dad passed by, he would smile and touch it.

Things were different, but I guess we found a way to be grateful for the time we spent together. Content that she was in the arms of the Lord, we moved on with our lives. That's why this is doubly hard. When I saw how my father was hurting that day, I went over to him and pulled on his robe. He sat down on a chair and pulled me up on his knee.

"Hey there, son of mine," he said, holding back tears. "How are you doing, kiddo?"

"I miss Mom," I said, plain and simple as an eight-year-old boy could.

"Is she coming back?" I guess I knew the answer to that question, but it was my frail attempt to make conversation.

"Oh no, my boy; Mommy isn't coming back. She's gone to join Grandma and Granddad."

"But Grandma and Granddad were old people; why did Mother have to join them now?" Dad smiled. I wasn't very tactful.

"Well, son, it was just her time. She got ill, and no matter which doctors we brought in or how many prayers we made, it was just her time. The Lord wanted her home. Think of it this way, my boy. With all the wealth we have, the nice home, servants, and food enough to last a lifetime, I believe the Lord looked down and decided that with all the love we had for Mother, He loved her more, and He could take care of her far better than we ever could. This world was just not good enough to treat her the way she deserves, so He took her home."

"But Dad, we miss her."

"Yes, my boy, of course we do. But always remember, she is happy where she is, and know every day when you wake up that your mother loves you. It's just that our heavenly Father has a bigger job for her to do with Him."

"Bigger than taking care of us?" Now when I look back, it did sound a bit selfish.

"Yes, my boy, bigger than taking care of us." He smiled and hugged me.

"If that is the case," I said reflectively, trying to sound all grown up, "then Father, I will never do anything to make you hurt this way again."

And now I realize I broke that childhood promise in the worst possible way. I remember it like it was yesterday.

"Hey, Dad."

"Hello, son of mine. What can I do for the distinguished son of the house?" He was smiling when he spoke. His eyes glistened. His eyes often glistened when he looked at my brother or me. It was as if he was always proud of us. I really didn't understand it.

My brother was a worker. Since we were a couple years apart, he had his friends and people in his age group he hung out with. I was just a younger generation.

We got on okay I guess; there was no animosity between us. It was just a matter of same father, different sons. Maybe he took after Dad and I took after Granddad; who knows.

I remember the conversation that followed. I got defensive and ruthless, blaming Dad for not allowing me to explore the world and see what was out there. All I knew was the inside of the family home. I wanted to have my own adventures and live my own life. After all, wasn't it my life to live?

I could see the hurt and disappointment growing on his face. My words were pointed like a dagger, each one stabbing more and more into his heart until finally, he gave in. He gave me what I wanted; I said my good-byes and left with the next set of traders that stopped at the home.

It didn't take long before I lost everything. I had bad taste in friends, my desires were short term, and it was all about me. And now the only job I could find was to feed the very animal our laws said we were to avoid.

Wow … how did I end up like this?

Well, I had a choice to make. I could continue to live like this or I could swallow my pride and go back home. When I thought of what I'd taken for granted, I threw away a life many people could only dream of.

My dad treated everyone around him with respect. I remember talking to his head servant in charge of the house, and I asked him if he ever got a chance to leave. He said yes, he could leave at any time with his master's blessing, but when he considered how good life was for him here, how would he be able to earn that level of security and peace on his own?

My dad had a gift, "favor from above," the servant called it. "That is not something that everyone has," he explained. "If you are fortunate to be under the umbrella of someone who's receiving the blessings of the Lord, then doesn't it stand to reason that you would partake of those same blessings?"

Oh man, even the servants were wiser than me. But if I turned back now, what would my Father say? Would he curse me and run me off? Maybe he'd already disowned me. I would. No, that wasn't him. Dad wasn't like that at all. I'd take my chances and go back. If anything, to live life like a servant was a lot better option than to live like this.

My heart was heavy the whole journey home. When I looked up and saw the house, I cringed as I remembered the hurt I had caused. And then I saw him running toward me. I stopped with my head hung down. He caught me and hugged me, crying and laughing at the same time. I couldn't say a word.

"Dad."

"Yes, son of mine."

I squeezed my eyes to hold back the tears, but they were already streaming down my face. "Dad … I'm sorry. I'm so sorry." I could barely speak. "Please forgive me … I'm so sorry."

"My boy, my lovely, beautiful boy, I forgave you a long, long time ago."

I looked up at his face and managed to give a relived smile. Then as he looked down at me, I could feel the love in his eyes as he spoke with a soft smile.

"After all, kiddo …

In The Middle of a Fire

Then King Nebuchadnezzar leaped to his feet in amazement and asked his advisers "Weren't there three men that we tied up and threw into the fire?" (Daniel 3:24)

"Ahhhhhhhhhhhhhhhhhh!"

"Well, that didn't sound very nice." Abed didn't talk much, but when he did he had a way of saying one liners that captured what we were thinking.

He was in front, and Shad was behind.

"I thought we were the only ones who stood up to the king." Shad had a good heart but he could be a bit naive at times.

"Shad, we are the only ones who stood up to the king," I confirmed to him. "The guys being burned are the guards who are feeding the fire."

"So why do they have to stand so close?"

Abed and I turned and looked at him and then turned away. It didn't make sense.

And then he opened his mouth again. "Meme."

"Yes, sir," I answered.

"Abed."

"I'm still here."

"Have you guys ever thought about dying?"

"He's talking to you, right?" said Abed, as if he was too drained to answer.

"Shad, isn't it a bit late to be thinking about that now?" I didn't know where he was going with this line of questioning, but I didn't want him to feel bad either.

"Hear me out, guys. I know we agreed not to bow down to the idol, right?"

"Right," confirmed Abed.

"And we decided that no matter what happened, we would stick together."

"Right again," I chipped in.

"And we believe that the Lord has the power to save us, but whether He chooses to or not, that's up to Him."

Abed turned and looked at me and gave a gentle smile.

"Well, my question is, are you afraid of dying? I know when we die we'll be going in to Abraham's rest, but what actually happens when you die?"

"Well," started Abed, "since I've never died before, I really don't have an answer for you."

"You know something," I said, thinking I should make a contribution to the discussion. "I'm not actually afraid of dying."

Abed looked at me with eyebrows lifted. "Really," he said in an amused kind of voice.

"No, I'm not," I said.

"As I was saying, before I was so rudely interrupted."

"Hummmm," Abed sounded, blowing through his nose.

"I don't think I'm afraid of dying but more afraid of the way I die."

"What do you mean?" asked Shad.

"Well, I'm not particularly fond of being burned alive."

"Understandable," chipped in Abed.

"Neither being hanged, stabbed, chopped up, pulled apart, crushed, or broken. I fear the suffering part of it. If I am to die, I hoped it would be at a ripe old age, lying in a bed fast asleep. You know—painless."

I felt satisfied with my answer.

"It sounds like a song," said Abed. "Let's give him a beat."

"Hanged, stabbed, chopped up, pulled apart, crushed, broken, broken, broken. Hanged, stabbed, chopped up, pulled apart, crushed, broken, broken, broken."

We sang together and found a catchy tune.

"Hey—shut up," shouted a guard.

"Why, what are you going to do, kill us?" shouted Shad.

We couldn't help it; we had to laugh.

"What about being eaten by lions?" asked Shad. "That must hurt."

Abed and I smiled and shook our heads.

Then Abed said the strangest thing. "All this waiting is making me hungry."

Now that he mentioned it, my stomach was growling a bit.

And then the guard told us that it was time. They led us down the corridor until we came to the main chamber. The king was standing near the wall with his advisors.

The guards led us in front of the king.

"Well," he said, "this is your final chance. If you bow down and worship the statue created in my honor then you can live."

"My king," Shad said first, "in myself I know I'm not the best gifted boy standing in front of you. Anything I have is an amazement to me because I know the power to do what I can do doesn't come from me; it comes from our God. I am not about to turn my back on Him because I've come across an adversity."

Then Abed stepped forward. "We stand together. We are friends in life, and we are friends in death. And as a matter of fact, my king, if I am to die today, I couldn't wish for any better company than my friends and brothers."

Abed turned to Shad and me and smiled.

"Know this, oh king," I said, "our God is greater than your supposed idol any day or time. Now we know that if it is His will, He will save us from that fire. But if He chooses not to and we perish, then we perish. Our decision is final. God is still God, so do your worst."

The furnace was built in the ground. It was a circular hole that had an iron step built on the side. My guess was that it was about twenty-five feet wide and thirty feet deep. Every time the guards went near to throw fuel into it, the flames burst up, flying in the air as the wood hit the bottom.

"Enough," shouted the king. "Tie them up tight and throw them in."

We looked at each other as we were being tied. Our mouths were closed, breathing through our noses. Sweat was pouring down our faces as the heat in the room was high.

We didn't fight or struggle. The ropes rubbed hard on my skin, and I could feel the pressure they put on me as they were tied tight. I could sense Abed and Shad were feeling the same thing.

And then it happened. Each of us was picked up at the same time, and then we took a final look at each other and nodded.

I closed my eyes and felt myself swayed back and then thrown hard in the air. I could feel myself flying, and I thought, *Well, I'll be dead before I hit the ground.*

I kept on floating. Then, as the force of the throw eased, I could feel myself falling. My mouth was pressed tight, and I breathed through my nose. Eyes still closed, I could feel the air brushing against my face; falling, falling. *Bump.* I hit the ground.

I lay there for a while until I heard a familiar voice.

"Meme." It was Shad. "Are you awake?"

"What kind of question is that?" I said, opening my eyes and standing up.

"What do you mean what kind of question is that—a question is a question."

"What do you say?" asked Shad, turning to Abed.

"Well … if you're not sleeping then you're awake, and if you're not dead, then you're alive."

Then it dawned on me. We were standing in the furnace. The ropes had come off us and we were all standing, but we weren't hurt.

None of us showed any signs of pain or burning. It's as if we were standing in a soft breeze of air.

"Now is this cool or what!" said Shad.

"Very," said Abed, smiling.

"Care to explain this?" another voice said.

"I don't know," I said to the young man.

"One minute we were being tied up on the surface, the next we were thrown in the furnace, and now, here we are. We're okay."

"Am … by the way, who are you?" I asked with a quizzical look on my face.

"Shadrach, Meshach, and Abednego." It was the king calling us. "I know I had three of you commissioned to be burned, but now I see a fourth man in the fire, having the form of the Son of God. Please, servants of the Most High, please come out of there."

We looked at the young man who shared the fire with us.

"Son of God?" asked Abed timidly.

"Absolutely," He said with a smile.

"This is so cool," said Shad, smiling.

I looked at my hands and body. The fire was burning, but I couldn't feel a thing.

"Come up," called the king again.

"Do we have to go?" questioned Abed, who was really enjoying himself.

"It's time, boys," said the young man. "You need to go. But don't you worry; things will get a lot better after this. Your Father has been watching you, and He's so proud. You've all done well."

We looked at each other, smiling freely.

"After all," said the young man, smiling,

Is This Magic?

Another of his disciples, Andrew, Simon Peter's brother, spoke up, "Here is a boy with five small barley loaves and two small fish, but how far will they go among so many?" (John 6:8–9)

I was in a special place. I felt as if, if I got beat up every day for the rest of my life, it wouldn't matter. Bullying was nothing new to me. Mind you, I could take the boys on in a one-on-one, but six to one—those odds were like working every day of the week until Sabbath; it was tough.

But right here, right now, it felt good.

A lot of people came to hear Him speak. My Mom and Dad had to work, but Mom wanted me to go.

"You may not get another chance to hear Him," she told me as she got me ready and packed a bag for me. "And besides, you might learn something."

By the time I got there, the place was full. There was hardly a place to sit. His voice carried through the air, and I could hear every word. Looking around I saw the boys who bullied me. They were with their parents, so they couldn't do anything. I wasn't afraid; I just wanted a fair fight.

And then, near the end of His speech, I could hear people murmuring about wanting to go home. We were in the hills, and it was a good distance to get back to the village. With so many people moving at the same time, it would be slow progress.

"Food, does anyone have any food?" the master's helpers cried out as they moved through the crowd. "The master is asking for anyone who has food to come forward."

People were talking and looking at each other. I guess nobody carried food because they didn't think they would be here that long. I recognized the helpers because they sat nearest to Him the whole time He spoke.

I looked around, carefully studying the crowd. Seriously—are you telling me that out of all the adults and children, nobody but nobody had anything! That was a bit hard to believe, but I guess it was true.

I was so busy looking at everyone else I forgot Mom had packed some stuff for me. I pulled the satchel bag from around my side and looked in. Wrapped in linen cloth were five loaves of bread and two fried fish.

"God bless you, Mother." I smiled and sat back. I could see the gang of boys looking at me with spiteful eyes. I just kept on smiling.

"Food, any food?" the call kept coming.

There must be someone with food. Of all these people around, no one had food? But someone did. I had some, and it was for me and me alone. And then a sudden feeling came over me. Ha, it was payback. To all the boys who bullied me and their parents for not teaching them to do better, plus the people who saw and did nothing; I was going to show them all.

I was going to eat my meal in front of everyone and make them suffer. After all, I couldn't feed all these people, so what difference would it make? I would have my revenge, even if it did last a few minutes. I could hit everyone with one blow. *Yes.* I was the man.

"Do you have any food, young man?" I was so taken up with myself I didn't see the man come up to me.

He asked again, "Do you have any food? The master is asking for any food."

Mom and Dad taught me that lying didn't bring happiness, and God would be disappointed in His children if they lied. Our house had a strong "don't lie policy."

But what could so little do for so many? I didn't want to disappoint my parents; after all, they had a way of hearing things. It's like they had special powers.

"Here sir," I said, getting up from my seat. "I have something."

"Thank you. Come with me, boy."

As he led me to the master, I could see the boys laughing at me. I guess they thought the same thing I thought—that my lunch was going to be taken so I would be in the same boat as them, as hungry as a church mouse.

"Come here, My child," the master said to me. "Sit here, right beside Me."

Although they had taken my lunch and were having a talk over it, I felt very special. I was sitting right beside Him. I pulled up my legs and put my arms around them, rocking back and forth gently and just looking up at His face.

I didn't hear everything, but I saw when He gave some commands to His helpers. They started going between the people and counting. I'm not sure of the number, but they were being separated into large groups and told to sit together.

All this time I was looking to see if anyone else had brought up food. Was the master going to eat my lunch Himself? It would be an honor, but I would still be hungry.

He waited and waited and waited. It took a while to get everyone together, and some people were not behaving nicely. Then He turned to me and smiled, and I smiled back. When people looked at Him, they also saw me. I was right in the scene.

Then He prayed. He prayed a blessing on the meal and the one He used to provide it. Hold on—the one He used to provide it. That's me—He prayed for me. Right then I didn't care that I had given up my meal or that I was going to go home hungry; I was thankful that He prayed a blessing for me.

Then what happened next I'm still not sure of. After the prayer He broke the fish and bread and placed pieces of each in baskets the helpers were holding. Then He said, "Go, but first take care of my little friend."

A helper came over to me and put his hand in the basket, and out came some fish and bread in his hand.

"Thank you, sir," I said, amazed

"Would you like some more?" he asked, smiling

"More?"

"Yes, more. You must be very hungry; it's been a long day. It's all right, there's plenty to go around."

I nodded, and he put his hand back in and pulled out fish after fish and bread after bread.

How could so little feed so many? I had to ask.

"Sir, how did you do that?" I asked the master, looking carefully at His sleeves.

"Well," he said reflectively, "do you believe you can make a difference in this world?"

I thought about the bullying, the odds against me, and the people who knew and did nothing.

"No, sir I can't. I'm too small to make a difference here."

"Well then, I guess the fish and bread came here by themselves."

"Of course not, master. You saw me bring them."

"Then you can make a difference," he confirmed. "Our Father was able to feed so many because you decided to make a difference."

Wow! I made a difference to thousands of people. The thought blew my mind.

"Your parents would be so proud of you today. After all, it pays not to lie."

I stood still in shock; how did He know!

"I think after this you'll be fine."

"How do You know, sir?"

"It's My job to know," He said, leaning into me. Then He smiled, winked at me, and walked away.

As I made my way down the hill, the guys were waiting for me. Then the leader came up.

"Well."

"Well what?"

"How did He do it? You were right there, so tell us."

"Yeah, yeah," the others started in a chorus.

I raised my hand for them to stop. "At first I thought it was magic," I said, "but now I believe it was a miracle."

That night I lay in bed, thinking about everything that had happened; all I could do was smile. "Thank You, Lord for blessing me today; I made a difference in my village, my bullies became my friends, I didn't lie, and on top of that, I was blessed by the master."

Then in the stillness of the night, a calming voice replied,

My Imaginary Friend

Now Samuel did not yet know the Lord: The word of the Lord had not yet been revealed to him. A third time the Lord called, "Samuel!" And Samuel got up and went to Eli and said, "Here I am; you called me." (1 Samuel 3:7–8)

"One, two, three, four, five, six, seven, eight, nine, ten, eleven …"

"Squeak."

"What's the matter with you? Didn't I just give you something to eat? How could you be hungry already?"

"Squeak … Squeak."

"How can your little stomach be so empty? Okay, okay here you go. But that's enough for tonight or you won't get any sleep."

"All right, let's try this again. One, two, three, four, five, six … six … six … six …"

Things weren't so bad during the day, but at night when I laid down to sleep, it really got lonely except for "mousey," who I'd found the other day.

I looked at the ceiling and tried counting the tiles again. "One … two … three …" It was no use. Why did I feel like this?

There was an ache in my stomach. I felt so tired, and I couldn't stop crying. Sometimes the crying put me to sleep, but tonight I really felt bad.

"Mom …" I knew she wasn't there, but anytime I felt ill, she was the person I called, and she always came. Deep breath in, "Harrrrrrr" … and out, "Wooooooo." Deep breath in, "Harrrrrrr" … and out, "Wooooooo."

I'd been living at the temple for some time now; I'm really not sure how long. It could have been a few weeks, but that didn't stop the pain from easing. Being homesick doesn't have a time limit.

Even though Mother had told me since I was born that I was going to stay here with the priest, nobody had any idea what living at the temple was going to be like. I remember what she used to say.

"Samuel."

"Yes, Mom."

"I need you to know something. Before you were born, I promised the Lord that if He gave me someone special, then I would give him back to Him."

"What does that mean?" No matter how often I heard it, I still couldn't understand.

"Well, it means you won't be living with Daddy and me."

"Mommy, don't you want me anymore?"

"Of course I do. I will always want you. It's just that you have a very special job to do. The priest will be your guide, and you will be his helper. Mommy and Daddy will come and visit you every chance we get."

"Mommy, I don't understand. Is the priest my father?"

"No, no, my son. Mommy and Daddy—we are your parents, and we will always love you."

Every time she talked to me about me leaving home, she cried. It was like she was happy and sad at the same time.

"So, Mom, when I'm at the temple, will I have any friends?"

"You are a good boy, and I'm sure you will be fine."

When I started at the temple, I found myself in a classroom of one. One time I asked Eli the priest, "Where are the other children?"

"You are the only one here," he said in a stiff, formal way.

"Sir, is that good or bad?" I was trying to understand why I was given away by my parents. Did I do something bad and couldn't stay at home? I missed my home. I felt safe at home.

"Hmmm … I know this must be difficult for you, but try and understand. Your parents—particularly your mother—want what's best for you."

"Isn't that to be with my family?" I asked in a very simple way.

Eli took a deep breath, and for the first time I could recall, he looked at me with a kinder, more tender sort of face. It was not like he was looking at his sons, who were big enough men, but when he looked at me, I actually felt he was looking at me—an eight-year-old boy who was lonely.

"Am … Samuel." I got the feeling Eli wasn't used to talking to children. "Sometimes parents make very difficult decisions, like what's best for their children. I can understand how you might feel abandoned, but please, don't take your being here as a negative thing. Your parents love you very much, and because of that love, they want to give you every opportunity to fulfil your purpose in life.

"You have been given a gift, my boy—the gift of finding your godly purpose and the opportunity to discover your potential from a very early age. Don't be afraid of this gift; embrace it, own it, and keep it.

"Your parents made a big sacrifice in letting you stay here because they know no other child will ever have the fulfilment you will find by staying at the temple." Eli looked tired.

"So being here is a good thing?" I asked him.

"For you it's the best thing." He smiled at me. "Now off to bed, young man. We have a lot to do tomorrow."

I did feel better after we talked, but I still had trouble sleeping at nights. I don't know when it happened, but finally I fell fast asleep.

First Call

"Samuel, Samuel, wake up, child."

"Who's there?"

I opened my eyes, yawned, and sat up, leaning back on my hands. Looking around I could see through the top window that it was still dark outside.

I wonder if it was Eli. It must have been. Nobody else was there. What could he want at this time of night?

I got out of bed, took a match, and striking it against the wall, lit my candle on the bedside table. I walked out the room and through the corridors to Eli's room. I was tired and not thinking clearly, so I went straight in, right up to his bed.

"Eli, I am here now. You called me, sir?" I was rocking from side to side, trying to stay awake.

Slap. I hit him. I couldn't wait any longer for him to wake up.

"What in heaven's name are you doing, boy, trying to kill me in my sleep?"

"You called me."

"No I didn't."

"Yes you did. I heard a voice call my name, 'Samuel, Samuel, wake up, child.'"

"Have you been imagining things, boy? Your loneliness has gotten the better of you."

"If it wasn't you, then who? Who else lives in the temple?"

He looked at me and shook his head slightly. "Go back to sleep. We'll talk about this in the morning. Hmmmm … just … go back to sleep."

Eli gave a tired smile and turned back into bed, pulling his covers over him.

Second Call

"Samuel, Samuel, wake up, child."

I opened my eyes but stayed in bed. Was I dreaming? I wondered if I was making it up. But it sounded so real, like a person; it must be Eli calling me. Well, he was getting old; maybe he didn't remember? I made the journey to Eli's room again, and sure enough, he was sleeping. *Nice.* I thought. *Now he's the one sleeping and I'm awake.*

"Eli, sir, please, I can't be doing this all night. If you have something to say to me, please remember so you don't have to call me again."

"Boy." He didn't sound amused. "What do you think you're doing waking me up in the night like this—again?" He was getting serious.

"Sir, I'm sure I heard you call. The voice was as clear as any other. If it wasn't you, then who was it?" I asked, shrugging my shoulders.

"For the last time, go back to sleep. I have a good mind to—" Eli stopped himself and took a deep breath.

"Samuel, I know things have not been easy for you settling in here and all, but please go back to sleep. We can talk about this in the morning."

One thing I don't like is when I tell the truth and people don't believe me. "Yes, sir," I said. There was no point in going on.

Third Call

"Samuel, Samuel, wake up, child."

Oh boy, I thought. *If this isn't him, I'm going to be in serious trouble.*

"Sir, sir, can I help you?"

"Samuel," Eli said in a voice of disbelief. This time he sat up, rubbed his eyes, and looked at me carefully. "Tell me, boy, what exactly did you hear?"

"Well, I was sleeping, and then I heard a voice calling me."

"Anything else?"

I thought for a moment, trying to see if there was something I missed. "Well," I started, "it sounded as if it came from within my room—and it was nice."

"Nice?"

"Yes, sir, it was a nice voice. I didn't feel afraid or anything. Maybe that's why I thought it was you. You have a nice voice too!"

Eli smiled and nodded his head while looking at his legs, as if to hide his face from me.

"Tell you what," he finally said, raising his head. "The next time you hear the voice"—he used his fingers to make quotation marks—"say these words: 'Speak, Lord, for thy servant heareth.'"

"Speak, Lord, for thy servant heareth," I repeated.

"Yes, just like that." He smiled.

That night the voice came again, and I repeated the words Eli had told me to say. The Lord spoke to me and gave me many instructions and plans for things to come. Some were good, and some didn't sound very nice.

"Lord," I started, "what you have told me is very difficult to say. How will I know what to say and to whom? And who will believe me anyway? This sounds like so much to be given to a boy like me." Then I remembered Eli's words. Maybe this was my godly purpose, my gift.

"Will you be with me, Lord, as I say these things?"

"I will always be with you, Samuel. Just remember, for now and forever more …

The Boy Wonder

When his parents saw him, they were astonished. His mother said to him, "Son, why have you treated us like this? Your father and I have been anxiously searching for you." "Why were you searching for me?" he asked. "Didn't you know I had to be in my Father's house?" (Luke 2:48–49)

"Well, if He's not in here, I don't know where else to look." As Mary and I passed through the corridor that led to the worship area of the temple, two young priests were at the other end walking toward us. "Let's ask them," said Mary. "They might have seen Him somewhere." She took the lead and beckoned to them.

"Excuse me, excuse me, sirs. Good day to you."

"And to you, madam."

"Can you help us? We're looking for our son. He's about twelve years of age, dark brown hair, and loves the temple."

Both priests looked at each other and gritted their teeth with a slight anxious smile.

"Sir, my lady," the one nearest to us said. "I think you'll find Him in the inner court. He's a … interesting young man." That did not sound good to me.

"Oh, thank you," said Mary smiling. I looked at her and wondered if she didn't realize what was going on.

"Yesssss," the priest continued. "He has been here for quite a while. It seems He's lost track of time."

"We've been looking for Him for a few days now," I volunteered. "At first we thought He was staying with relatives after the Passover, but we contacted everyone we knew and He has been missing for some time."

"Well, He's been here, and He's been very entertaining with his thoughts on the Scriptures. Tell us, where did He get such training and understanding of the laws? He must have a teacher. Who has been coaching Him?"

I looked at Mary, but she was selectively quiet and just gently shook her head.

"I don't think He has received any more teaching than what has been given by the priests. Maybe He's just a good learner?"

"Maybe," the young priest said, unconvinced. "Anyway, take our advice. You had better go in there and take your son out." He looked more serious now. His voice seemed to have more concern than amusement. "Your son has a gift, and the high priest does not like to be shown up in his own court. Take my word for it."

He pressed his lips into a smile and nodded, and they both left. Mary and I looked at each other. We had an idea of what was coming.

The high priests were the leaders of the temple and supposed spiritual guides of the people. But there was also the other side of them. It was known that if one got on their wrong side, they held great influence with the Romans, and for a price, they could pay them to do their, let's just say … unpleasant bidding.

We continued down the corridor and entered in to the main worship area of the temple. We could see Jesus standing in the middle of the court, speaking to it seemed a dozen priests, and the high priest was there looking at Him intently.

"Was man made for the Sabbath or the Sabbath for man?"

"What sort of question is this the boy asks?"

"Should we answer Him?"

"Man was made for the Sabbath … wasn't he?"

"No, no the Sabbath was made for man … I think."

"Who is your teacher, boy?" the high priest said, joining the conversation.

"God is my teacher."

Oooooooh wrong answer, Jesus. What are you doing, son? You're supposed to be slipping out of trouble, not going deeper into it. I had to find a way to get him out without intimidating the high priest.

I was about to make a step forward when I felt Mary's hand hold my arm.

"I know Jesus can take care of Himself," she said in a calm, quiet voice, "but I know how you are when it comes to him. Be careful, my love. We've seen what the high priest is capable of. Promise me you won't do anything foolish."

"Me, foolish? I'm the most sensible man you know. That's why you married me, remember!" I smiled, trying to make light of the situation. Mary managed to muster a half smile back.

"Good day, sirs," I said, stepping forward. "Please, allow me to apologize for my son. Sometimes He doesn't know when to stop. He loves the temple and the Lord, but I hope He hasn't been an inconvenience to you."

"So, you are the boy's father?" The high priest took center stage to represent the order. My eyes quickly picked up that the other priests became deafeningly quiet. By their body language I could sense they had retired their arguments and questions to allow the high priest to speak uninterrupted.

"Well, are you the boy's father or not?"

"Yes, I am."

Although we were in the temple, I could sense a dark presence surrounding the room, like something was moving in the atmosphere.

Mary went in for the save.

"Jesus," she called, "where have You been, son? We have been looking for You everywhere."

"Didn't you know I would be about My Father's business?"

I closed my eyes and breathed out quietly; "wrong answer again."

"Father's business?" the high priest repeated. "I thought you said you were His father."

"Yes, I did … and I am."

"Then what sort of nonsense is this the boy speaks?" The high priest was beginning to get very aggravated, as if someone was trying to make him look bad.

"I may not understand everything my son does and says—and that can make life a bit difficult at times—but He's my boy and my responsibility."

Playtime was over.

"Jesus."

"Yes, Dad?"

"It's time to go, son. Come and stand here with your mother."

My voice was calm and low, but I could feel the heat rising in my head.

"I asked you a question, peasant." His voice was demeaning.

By now the other priests were watching intently to see who would lose their temper first.

"What is your occupation?"

"I am a carpenter," I said, not being intimidated by his robes or position.

"Then how can a carpenter afford such teaching for a boy of His age?"

"Is it my fault a boy can discuss legal matters with our most distinguished leaders and leave them confounded?"

The high priest rose up quickly and stepped briskly, stopping within inches of my face. "You had better watch that tongue of yours, peasant. You might lose it before the day is ended."

Then I heard a familiar voice speak to me in my head. "Now is not the time."

I thought intently for a moment. "Then I guess my tongue and I should best be leaving."

The priests started laughing; but the high priest still looked at me, determined not to back down.

"Sir, it's getting late and we need to confirm the plans for evening prayers," said the young priest we'd met in the corridor, walking toward us. The high priest looked at him and then turned his attention back to me.

"Yes, yes, the evening prayers," he said with a smile. But his smile was not genuine, I could tell. "You should bring the boy again someday. It would make for an interesting discussion."

He nodded slightly, and I returned the gesture. Then he turned and left with the young priest, and they both disappeared through a side exit.

I placed my left hand on my chest and bowed slightly to the priests who were sitting on the steps like spectators at a game. They nodded their heads in acknowledgment, and then I returned to Mary and Jesus.

Walking toward them, I said, "It's time to go."

Walking through the corridor, Jesus looked up at me. I was thinking about the high priest.

"I don't think we're safe here."

"Should we relocate?" Mary asked me.

"Let's see what the Lord says. If He wants us to go, He'll have no problem telling us, that's for sure."

"Dad."

"Yes, Jesus."

"Are you angry with me?"

"Why would You ask that, boy?"

"The look on your face—that's why," said Mary, smiling.

"No, of course not, son; You've done nothing wrong for us to be upset about. In fact, if we had realized it earlier, we would have come to the temple first. Don't You worry, boy. It will be okay."

"Are you sure, Dad?"

"Of course I am. After all, Jehovah is Your Father."

Then looking at him, I said, smiling, "But …

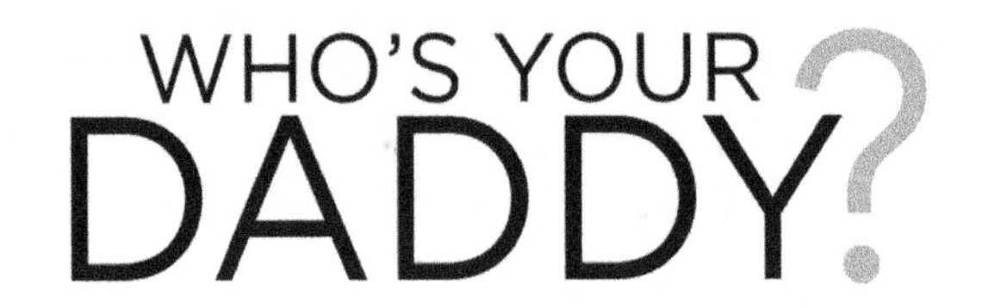

The Choice

(Jonathan son of Saul had a son who was lame in both feet. He was five years old when the news about Saul and Jonathan came from Jezreel. His nurse picked him up and fled, but as she hurried to leave, he fell and became disabled. His name was Mephibosheth.) (2 Samuel 4:4)

Today looked like any other day to me. I was fortunate to have my bed placed near the window in my room. The house where I lived now had two stories and was a lot nicer than the one we lived in before.

Don't you just hate it when what people can do naturally is a struggle for you? Just to pull myself up to the window ledge so I could look outside had become the toughest job for me to do. Trying to use my feet—forget that. I wasn't the jealous type; I really wasn't. It's just that … well, when I see boys playing outside on the street, I don't think badly of them for being able to do it, but why me?

Why should I have to be the one stuck in this prison of a room when I can see people walking? Can you imagine a thing like walking—something so basic that so many people take for granted? I would love to know what it's like to feel sand and dirt between my toes, to feel the ground beneath my feet, and to actually feel water against my feet and not just wash in it. I would give anything. Hold on—I'm poor, remember. What do I have to give? Give anything—yeah right.

I've been told by my carers that I was dropped as a baby boy, and when my feet hit the ground, my leg bones and nerves were shattered. Since then I was dependent on someone to carry me around. I may have been dropped in body, but I feel like I was dropped in mind and spirit too.

Usually when I heard people speak of their generation, they would use the term "the son of." 'The son of' was a way of linking fathers and sons and what they did. The story I heard was I was once a prince. Can you believe it, me … a prince? I was told my grandfather was the first king of Israel, King Saul. They say he was the tallest man ever, that he stood head and shoulders over all the people. I can't even stand up. Then there was my father, the crown prince and love of the people, Prince Jonathan.

There are no crowds who chant my name and love me. Why did I have to lose everything?

Looking through the window, I saw someone who looked different from the regular travelers. He was asking for directions, and people were pointing him to our home.

He looked very well dressed in fine robes of purple and white, and I saw half a dozen soldiers following behind him keeping pace. There was a knock at the door, and then I pulled myself off the ledge and onto the bed.

I was so curious to find out what was going on I rolled off the bed and crawled to the door. I managed to crack it open just in time for my carer to answer the door.

"Hello, can I help you?"

"Good day, sir. My name is Ziba. Are you Machir?"

"Yes, I am. Come in, come in. What can I do for you?"

"I have been commissioned by the king to find any remaining children of Jonathan, son of the late King Saul. King David's desire is to restore favor to their household. Is there a young man here by the name Mephibosheth?"

"Yes, sir, Mephibosheth lives here under our care."

"Then bring him. The king is anxious to meet him. We cannot delay, and we have no time to waste."

Machir came to my room and caught me on the ground.

"I guess you heard."

"Does the king want to kill me?"

"No, no. David and Jonathan were the best of friends. They were a lot closer than King David was with his own brothers I think …" he said in a reflective tone while helping me up to sit on my bed. "The Lord has heard our prayers, and things are going to be different from now on."

And then, for the first in a long time, we both smiled and gave a chuckle.

The palace was beautiful. The walls were decorated with colorful designs and shining stones. Was this to be my new home? It was too much to take in.

We were led in by the guards who came for us out of the city. The journey itself was long, but the excitement of going to the palace made everything else seem distant.

But there was a problem, or at least I thought so. I was in a wonderful palace, the opposite of Lodebar. Everyone was dressed in fine clothes and looked so prim and proper.

But I was still wearing my worn-out clothes, and my condition hadn't changed. I was still a cripple.

I was escorted into the main hall. I could use my crutches for short distances but had to be carried otherwise.

And then the King entered the room. With my crutches under my arms, I pressed up to balance on my feet.

He looked good. If you ever imagined what a king looked like, it was King David. His crown was shining gold, his hair and beard well groomed. His robe was blood red with golden trimmings and designs. There was no mistaking who he was.

Then he spoke. "Don't be afraid, my boy. I didn't bring you here to harm you. Your father and I were the best of friends."

His voice was tender. It was strange. He looked so majestic, so powerful, and yet in his voice I could sense his compassion and warmness. I felt safe.

"All the land that your family owned will be restored to you. You will not have to suffer any more. As a matter of fact, from now on, I want you to live in the palace and dine at my table with the other princes. Your suffering days are over. All your needs will be provided for from this day forth."

Did men cry? Were men allowed to cry? All the men I'd been around either cursed, drank, swore, and fought for the smallest thing, like if someone stepped on their toes or bounced into them on the street by accident. I had never seen a grown man cry, but that day, when I looked up at the king, I could see tears slowly running from his eyes.

He didn't make a sound, and he didn't lose his posture, but the way he looked at me, it was as if he saw right through me. I felt as if he wasn't just talking to me; he was talking to my father and grandfather. He was speaking to my past and my future. It was too much.

"Who am I, my king? I'm a nobody; I have about as much use as a dead dog. I don't deserve this; I don't deserve any of this." I fell to the ground and cried. I couldn't hold it in any longer.

Then he came over to me, and kneeling down, he placed his hand on my shoulder.

"My boy … Mephibosheth, what in the world happened to you? I can't tell you the Lord will make you walk again. That is in His hands. But there is one thing I do know—you don't have to have a broken body to have a broken spirit. He is a healer—of lives torn by war, people suffering the loss of loved ones, and hearts that have gone through so much pain that one more day just will not do. Give Him your pain. He can trade your sorrow for gladness and give you a crown of beauty instead of ashes, the oil of joy instead of mourning, and a garment of praise instead of a spirit of despair."

After he had given some orders to his officers, making arrangements for my new reinstated wealth, I was shown my room. I had a view with a balcony that over looked the city.

In one day, I went from looking out my window to the streets of the ragged, poor town where I lived to the palace. From here, everything I knew before looked so small.

"Your Highness." I turned around on the chair I was sitting in, and a young man was standing in the middle of the room.

"I am Tama, and I will be your servant here at the palace. We need to get you ready for dinner. The king wants to introduce you to the other princes. This is big, sir. It would be good if you made a good first impression."

Tama helped me bathe, and then he laid out my dinner clothes.

"Is this what I wear for dinner?"

"You're in the palace now, sir. You will find things run a bit different here," he said with a smile. "Don't worry; I won't leave your side. But watch out—one or two of the fellow princes can be a little cheeky. By the way, the king's engineers had an invention made for you. I'll get it now."

Tama soon returned with a royal chair but with chariot wheels attached to each side. Army shields were placed on the inner circles of the wheels. There was a flat step across the front so I could keep my feet off the ground and small wooden wheels attached to each side of the step to stabilize the larger wheels.

"I can push it, and it will make it easier for you to move through the palace. It doesn't take corners so well, but in time I think you should be able to maneuver it on your own."

I sat in my chair with wheels, and putting my hands on the large wheels, I pushed myself toward a mirror. I could hardly recognize myself—wearing a prince's clothes, well groomed, and sitting in a royal; I don't know what name they gave it except "wheelchair." Yes, sitting in my royal wheelchair.

Looking at my reflection, I had a choice to make. I could live in the palace, have a restored inheritance, eat at the king's table, be crippled, but choose to be happy, and who knows, maybe fall in love and have a family of my own one day.

Or I could live in the palace, have a restored inheritance, eat at the king's table, and be crippled … and continue to feel sorry for myself, blaming everyone else for my condition.

We made our way to the dining table. It was very long. I didn't realize the king had so many children. Some were princes; some were not directly in line to the throne. Then there were the mothers and daughters. I let out a low breath as we came near to the table.

"Be cool, be cool," I could hear Tama say. I think he was more nervous for me than I was for myself.

Then the king beckoned me to sit at the corner across from him. As I got close to the table, the prince sitting there got up and said, "Hey, Mephibosheth, take my chair."

"Oh, no thanks," I said, smiling. "I like to travel with mine." Everyone burst out with laughter, even the king.

I chose to be happy.

Around the dinner table, everyone looked equal. No one asked about my legs. They didn't even bring it up. Pushed under the king's table, my condition was covered. It was still there for sure, but somehow it didn't make a difference as to who I was or my position at the table.

The king looked over at me and asked, "Is everything all right for you?"

"It's a lot better than I could ever have imagined," I replied

"Good, good," he said. "I miss your father. He was my best and closest friend. You know, son, if there's anything you need, don't be afraid to come to me, even if it's just to talk."

"Thank you, sir. I'll keep that in mind."

"After all, right now, right here …

The Living Sacrifice

Then God said, "Take your son, your only son, whom you love—Isaac—and go to the region of Moriah. Sacrifice him there as a burnt offering on a mountain I will show you." (Genesis 22:2)

Come on—I may not be the brightest spark, but I know I'm not stupid. I could tell something was wrong before we even left our home. Mother doesn't cry for nothing. And there she was hugging and kissing me as if she wasn't going to see me again. Get a grip, Mom. I'm only going with Dad to make a sacrifice. It's not like we haven't done this before. What made this time so special anyway?

I was curious as to where we were going, though. I didn't think I'd ever taken this route before. When I asked Dad where we were going, he just said, "I'll know it when I see it."

Well I guess there was nothing else to do but hope he knew where he was going. Sometimes my dad could be funny like that. It seemed he had a habit of going places he'd never been before. Mind you, it did make for some interesting travel. At least it added a little suspense and mystery to the journey.

But now this was getting out of hand. I was beginning to get a little annoyed. Just think of it—finally we came to the base of the mountain, and now I was thinking, *Yes, we're here. We can make up camp and do what we need to do.* But then my dad gave a strange order. He told the helpers to unload the donkeys—fair enough—and gather sticks for the sacrifice. That sounded reasonable, but then he said they had to stay with the animals while he and I started the final leg of the journey up the mountain.

You know something—it's in times like these I missed Mom, because really, Dad could be a difficult person to talk to at times. I loved him to bits, I really do, but when he got like this, it was as if you were talking to a brick wall trying to get information out of him.

So let's try this again. "So, Dad."

"Isaac, what is it? I'm kind of busy right now."

Okay then … kind of busy … walking up a mountain. Interesting.

This conversation was going nowhere fast. One more time. "Ummmm, Dad, you know … you know you said we were going to make a sacrifice, right?"

"Yes, I remember. I said that."

"Well then." I paused for a while. The more I talked, the more confused I felt. "Well, correct me if I'm wrong, but we have the firewood, right? And we have the flint to start a fire. But don't you think we're missing something here? Isn't there supposed to be a sacrifice for the … well … sacrifice?"

"My boy, my son, God Himself will provide a sacrifice."

Now I was really confused. We were there to sacrifice something to God, which He was going to give us in the first place? Then why did we need to make a sacrifice if God already had the thing He wanted us to give to Him? Why didn't He just keep what He already had?

My logic and reasoning ability couldn't figure this one out. Hold on a minute. What were the facts of this mystery? What was I missing here?

To begin with, Mom was crying her eyes out as if she wasn't going to see me again. Second, Dad told the helpers to stay with the donkeys as only he and I would go up the mountain. Third, we had sticks for the burning and flint to start the fire. This didn't sound good. I started to get a sick feeling in my stomach.

I looked at Dad, and it dawned on me; he hadn't smiled once since we left the camp. Usually he was talkative when we were journeying together. It was like our bonding time. Maybe that's what really made the journeys so interesting. It wasn't so much the places we went to but rather the discussions we had along the way.

I squeezed my eyes tight and began to breathe deeper and deeper. I was trying to remain calm. I looked up at him again, and I could see he had a worried look on his face. I pressed my lips into a smile. I think in a way I was trying to cheer him up.

I took another deep breath and looked around me. The ground was getting more steep and rocky. I looked back and could sense we had passed the mark where one might expect a ram or goat to climb. It wasn't their usual habit to climb this high up a mountain.

I walked and held my head down. It was me; I was the sacrifice.

Oh boy. This one really stank. No wonder Dad had that look on his face. I took another deep breath.

"The Lord told you to do this, didn't He?" Dad didn't answer. We continued walking in silence.

Then my dad spoke. "We're here."

In silence we unpacked the bags and laid out the wood. Tears started to come to my eyes when I saw the long, broad knife come out of a bag. It glistened in the sunlight as if to introduce the world to my death.

"Dad, I don't understand it, and even if I were to ask you to explain, I guess it wouldn't make sense to me either."

"My boy, my lovely, lovely boy—if He had asked for my life I would have given it in an instant. There would be no need for this. But God has not asked for me; He's asked for you."

"Yes, but Dad, if there was another way, couldn't we take it?"

"The only way is if God provides it Himself. But this is what He told me to do."

My dad was crying so hard. I resigned myself to the fact that God wanted to call me home to Him. It wasn't my first choice, but it was my surrendered one.

I lay down on top of the sticks, carefully placed on the flat stone we had chosen. As my father tied my hands and feet one by one, I closed my eyes and thought of my mother and my friends. I began to breathe through my nose and allowed my body to go limp. Just then the strangest thing happened.

I felt a sense of peace overcome me that I had never felt before. It was as if a spirit of calmness touched me, starting from my head and passing through my body to my feet. I almost started to smile. Then I opened my eyes.

"It's all right, Dad; you need to do what God has told you. I will be just fine," I said with a smile. I looked at him crying and shaking his head. At that moment I felt as if I could never love him more than I did right then as he broke down because of what was going to happen to me.

My father was about to sacrifice me—his only son—to God, and the feeling that filled my heart wasn't anger, malice, or rage. It wasn't bitterness, judgement, or condemnation.

It was love. Love for my mother, love for my father, and thankfulness. I found myself thanking God for the gift of life—for the time I had spent on this earth, no matter how brief. It was good.

"Okay, Lord," I breathed. "Into Your hands I commend my spirit." My eyes were closed, and I waited.

"Abraham, Abraham, do not harm the child, for now I know you are a friend of God."

The voice was loud. It sounded as if it came from above, like a force rushing down from the sky. I waited and waited. Nothing happened. Something else was said, but I didn't get it. I was in a sort of daze from the first command.

Then I could feel my father pulling quickly at the knots for my hands. I opened my eyes and saw him crying and drawing deep breaths of relief. After untying my hands, he grabbed me and held me close for a good while, rocking from side to side while rubbing the back of my head with his right hand. His left was pressing on my back, hugging me tight. It was as if he never wanted to let me go again.

"Come on, boy, there's something we've got to do before we go." He untied my feet, and then over in a bush we saw a ram caught by the horns.

It puzzled me for a while to see him there. Where did this animal come from? And then as if on cue, my father's words came back to me: "God himself will provide a sacrifice."

You know what? No more questions. "Lord, thank You for Your provision.'

I don't know how and I don't know when, and as a matter of fact, I don't even care.

All I know is, there was a sacrifice, and it wasn't me.

After we had done our duty, we headed down the hill.

"Dad."

"Yes, my son."

"Would you really have killed me?"

"Hmmmmm … only if I had to, like if you still kept your tent messy and caused your mother grief."

"Oh Dad, please …" I looked at him and smiled. Then for the first time today, he looked at me and smiled back.

That was the face—that was the face I knew.

"Hey, son of mine."

"Yes, Dad."

He rubbed my head and then pulled me under his arm.

Why Won't You Believe Me?

Then Moses and Aaron fell face down in front of the whole Israelite assembly gathered there. Joshua son of Nun and Caleb son of Jephunneh, who were among those who had explored the land, tore their clothes and said to the entire Israelite assembly, "The land we passed through and explored is exceedingly good." (Numbers 14:5-7)

"Come on, boy, try and keep up. If you slip, there's no guarantee I'm going to come back for you." This guy was fit. We were running through the forest, jumping over fallen trees, sliding under ones that were too big to jump over but had just enough space between the trunk and the ground for a body to slip through.

On top of that, he was laughing too. This was fun for him.

"Aren't you afraid?" I tried to get in before the next hurdle came.

"Afraid of what?"

"Giants," I shouted.

"Giants—why should I be afraid of giants?"

"No, giant—ten o'clock."

He glanced to his left and then straight ahead, keeping the same pace.

"Down here." He pointed to some boulders and then he slid on his legs and bottom until he reached them and took cover. I followed and did the exact same thing.

"You're a quick learner, boy," he said with a smile.

"You're not so bad yourself," I said, returning the compliment.

We peeped out by the side of the boulder and took a good look at these extraordinarily large people.

"Have you ever seen anyone like them before?" I asked, curious to get as much information as I could.

"Sorry, I'm afraid not," my companion said. "Look … see how slow they are. Possibly because of their size they find it hard to move around."

"If that's so," I added, "then we would have an advantage in a fight."

"I agree."

We waited and watched them pick up fruit and gather wood. They were around fifteen feet tall. Their arms were long but seemed out of sync with the rest of their bodies. It was as if their arms received instructions after the rest of their bodies started to move. They were muscular and broad. But my new friend and I believed we could still take them in a fight.

We retreated behind the boulder and compared notes.

"Do you notice something different about this land?"

"Yes I do," I said, "but I couldn't put my finger on it … I need another look."

Then turning to look around the other side of the boulder, I came face-to-face with the ugliest man I had ever seen in my life.

"Grrrrrrrrrrrr." He grinded his teeth, and I started to retreat. Moving backward, I kicked my partner, who was looking behind the other side of the boulder.

"What?" he said

"Run," I whispered

"Grrrrrrrrrrrr."

I couldn't understand it. How could he not hear the growling right in front of me? I kicked again, only this time harder.

"What?" he whispered louder, turning around. "Oh."

"Yes, oh," I said, fed up.

Then he turned around, jumped on my back, and with one foot pushed himself off to fly in the air. He caught the giant around the neck and began to choke him with an arm lock.

Well that's one thing I found out about my friend—he wasn't afraid to carry the fight to the enemy.

"What do you want me to do?"

"Don't kill him unless you have to. What we want is just to get away. This is supposed to be a sightseeing mission, not a way to start a war. We'll have fighting soon enough. Kick his knees."

I did as the older man said and kicked the knees of the giant. As he fell to the ground, holding his knees in agony, my friend used the opportunity to jump off the giant's back and land on his feet.

"Very good," he said. "Now let's go before his friends arrive."

We continued to spy the land. Occasionally we would run into others who were sent out with us. Then we realized what was so different.

It was the fruit.

When the giant was picking the fruit, it looked proportionate to his size. But now we were looking at it—the grapes, apples, and berries; everything grew larger in this land. Was the soil so rich that the vegetation could grow beyond the ordinary? We had to tell the others.

We met up with the other men. There were twelve of us who started out. Luckily all of us came back fine. We met back at the rendezvous point to decide on our next course of action.

"We need to get back to the people," my friend suggested, "but we needn't go back empty-handed."

"Did you see the size of those grapes?" another man volunteered.

"So what are we going to do?" another man asked.

"How about we go back carefully?" my friend suggested. "We go back, but this time in pairs, and pick a branch of any fruit we can carry. Besides, the bunches look too big for one normal-sized man to handle alone."

The idea seemed good and pleased everyone.

"Well boy, are you ready for the second leg?" he said, smiling.

"Only if you're willing to pay attention and not get us killed," I replied with a smile.

"Listen, kiddo … If I wanted us dead we would have been dead already."

That didn't make much sense to me at all, so I just brushed it off with a look that said, "Really!"

"By the way, what's your name, boy? I can't keep calling you boy now can I?"

"Well no, I hope not. I'm Joshua."

"My friends call me Caleb."

"Nice to meet you," I said with a smile

"Likewise. Let's get going."

After we collected our bounty, we regrouped and made our way back to the camp. Moses and the people were waiting.

"Let us welcome back our brothers," said Moses. The people cheered and clapped. It felt good to be appreciated.

"Rest for the night, my brothers, and tomorrow you can tell us how you fared in the land."

The people separated to their tents, and I rejoined my dad.

In the morning the people gathered outside the tabernacle of the congregation, the place where Moses meet and talked with God.

"My brothers and sisters, the land truly is a good land, one flowing over with milk and honey."

The reports about the land were good, and the people were getting enthused. I found Caleb, and we greeted each other warmly. I could only think that I had found a good friend.

But then as quick as a snake could come out of the sand, the news of the giants and the other tribes who lived in the land started to spread. The other ten men started spreading their fears. It was like catching a virus. Once it gets you, it spreads to your whole body.

Caleb got up. "People, people, listen to me. What our brothers say is true; yes, there are giants, and yes, other tribes live in the far areas. But the land is a good land, and if we believe God has given it to us for an inheritance, then we should go in and possess it."

"No! No!" were the shouts. "It would have been better for us to stay in Egypt. At least we knew where our food was coming from."

I couldn't take it anymore. "Brethren—my brethren, listen to us. Caleb speaks the truth. We've seen the giants. They are slow and clumsy. And as for the tribes, how many battles have we already won with the Lord on our side? And now as we stand on the brink of our promise, you choose to leave what the Lord has given you? No, brothers. Who will stand with us and take the land? It's waiting for us. Who will go … anyone?"

As I looked at the gathering, the people were angry. How could this happen? Yesterday the same people were cheering us as conquering heroes, but today, they wanted to cut our throats.

Well, there was one man I knew would want the people to go in and possess the land. My dad, Nun.

"Dad, Dad, you believe me, don't you? You believe the report of Caleb's and mine."

My dad stood there and said nothing. He looked at me, and then he looked at the angry people. In his heart I could see he made a choice. He didn't want to evoke the anger of the people by standing up for his son.

"Dad," I cried in a soft voice. If he didn't believe in me, then who did?

We didn't go in. The venture did not generate enough support, but what was going through my mind was my dad forsaking me when I needed him most.

"Joshua, what's wrong?" It was Moses.

I told him what refusing the promise of God meant for me. Not only was I without a portion of land to call my own, but now I was without a father. Although I forgave him, he wanted nothing more than to keep his distance from me.

Do young men cry? This one did. I was hurting, and I wept bitterly.

Then I felt Moses put his arm around me. "Young man."

"Yes sir."

"I'm not your father, but there is a lot of work to be done and I need you by my side."

"You, Moses … need me?"

"Well, yes I do. Will you follow me as I follow God?"

"Yes sir, I will."

"Just remember, lad, if I can do anything for you, just let me know. After all …" Moses said with a soft smile,

You Were My Responsibility

So when the Midianite merchants came by, his brothers pulled Joseph up out of the cistern and sold him for twenty shekels of silver to the Ishmaelites, who took him to Egypt. When Reuben returned to the cistern and saw that Joseph was not there, he tore his clothes. (Genesis 37:28–29)

Have you ever tried looking at the sun with your eyes closed? You can feel the heat against your face. Through my eyelids I could see colors of red, yellow, and purple. It always gave me a happy feeling. Sunshine makes me happy.

It's a pity I don't have more days like this. Almost everything I do at home seems to inflict anger or disgust with someone. Just the other day I was sharing with my family how I saw in a dream stars shining with the sun and moon present. Then all the stars bowed down to one particular star. And then there was another dream where stalks of hay were gathered together in a group and all the stalks bowed down to one particular stalk.

My family questioned if the dreams were saying that they would bow down to me one day. I didn't know for sure. The reason I shared the dreams in the first place was to ask them what they meant. There were twelve of us brothers; how could it be that they, including my mother and father, were to bow down to me? It didn't make any sense. I was trying to make sense of it all.

But for some time now things had been a bit tense, especially since my father had a colorful coat made for me. He knew I loved colors by the way I described things I saw each day. I think it pleased him the way I could see things differently than other people did.

Well at least I felt safe around Reuben, my oldest brother. He wasn't the strongest physically or even the smartest, for that matter, but my brothers and I respected him for his position in the family and his character as a person. He wasn't a bully like some of my brothers were. He always seemed to rest on the side of what was fair, and we usually agreed with his decisions in times of conflict when our father was absent.

"Joseph, what are you doing here?"

"Oh, hi there, Joel. Father sent me to look for my brothers and find out how they're doing." Joel was all right. He was a herder for my Father and worked with my brothers in the fields.

"Well I think they've gone over the northern range. It's a bit farther than usual, but if you follow the trail over that hill, you should catch up with them soon enough."

"Thanks, Joel."

"Don't mention it. Travel safe."

He smiled and was turning his back when I had to say it. "Joel."

"Yes, young master," he said with a smile.

"Thank you. You know, you're one of the few people I can talk to without feeling I've unknowingly done something against. I don't know if that makes any sense, but thanks."

"Joseph, I can only imagine what you're going through. Your dad loves you a lot. You know that, right?"

"Yes, but that's not the problem."

"I know. The issue here is how your brothers feel about you. You have something special, and some people will like you for it and some won't. The main thing is you stay true to who you are and no matter what, always keep your faith in God. He will help you navigate through life. And as for your brothers—well, don't be too hard on them; they'll come around in time."

"Thanks for that. I feel a lot better."

"You take care." And with that he was off.

I followed the trail and could see the herds and then my brothers farther in the distance. I called out to them and waved. Either they didn't hear me or they ignored my calling. I chose to go with "they couldn't hear me."

"Hello, brothers."

"What's he doing here? Did Father send you to spy on us?"

"What now—not even our own jobs he trusts us to do?"

"No, brothers, nothing like that. Father just wanted to know how you all were. That's all."

"Wants to know how we are doing—the only person I thought he cared about was you."

"Come on, my brothers, why be like this? Father loves all of us. He's just concerned for your safety, that's all."

"Enough of this. I'm tired of hearing the words of a dreamer."

"Yes, yes, it's time we put this dreamer in his place." I really didn't like the sound of that, and my heart started to race.

I could see the anger and disgust building in their eyes. Their words were cold and direct. This wasn't my imagination acting up; no, this was real.

"Get him." I tried to run, but they were too many and too fast to get away from. I felt hands grabbing my clothes and tearing them off.

"Stop this! What are you doing? I'm your brother."

"Not today you're not." They caught me and tied my hands around my back and pulled me back to the center of the camp.

"What's going on here?" Thank God I recognized that voice; it was Reuben.

"Father sent the dreamer to spy on us."

"Yes, and we've had enough of him."

"We say kill him."

"Yes, kill the boy; I don't want to bow down to any junior."

***

What was I going to do? Joseph could be a pain and there were times when I wish he would just keep his mouth shut, but killing him? He didn't deserve that. But I couldn't take them all on. He was the favored of us. I needed to do something.

"Don't kill the boy."

"Why not? Now is the perfect time to get rid of him."

"Yes, we can kill him and then tell Father he got lost or captured."

"No."

"Reuben, you need to decide whose side you're on. Are you with us or with him?"

I looked at Joseph; he was so scared, like a helpless lamb. Our eyes locked, and I could see he believed I was his only hope.

I, like all of us, knew Joseph was the apple of our father's eye, but that didn't matter right now. He was the eleventh, and I was the first; I had a duty and responsibility to all my brothers' safety and wellbeing. We all believed our father loved Joseph the most. Me, he had loved the longest.

Who do you value more?

It was time to grow up and get past how my father treated me. It was time to stop blaming Dad for how I felt and get a hold of who I was. I was Reuben, the eldest son of the sons of Jacob. That was who I was—the eldest son. It was time to make my play.

"My brothers, there is no need to have our brother's blood on our hands. Here is a pit; let us keep him there for now. He can do no harm there."

"Yes, yes I see. Okay, Reuben, let's do that."

One by one they agreed, and then they tore Joseph's coat off and threw him in a dug-out pit. The brothers were so bitter against Joseph; they didn't even give him water when he asked for some. I went over to the pit and leaned in.

"Joseph."

"Reuben, I'm frightened. I'm really frightened. Am I going to die?"

"No, I promise you, I will get you out of this. You just need to play along for a while. I knew how they felt but never thought it would come to this. Just stay here and give me some time. I'll sort it out."

***

Reuben pressed his lips into a smile, trying to reassure me that things would work out.

"Don't leave me here," I cried

"I'll be close; just don't say anything that will tick them off more than they already are. I'll be back soon."

I could hear my brothers eating and drinking as if nothing had happened. How could they act so cold? It was as if they had no consciences.

I don't know how much time had passed, but I could hear the hoofs of camels in the distance, and then I heard a voice. It wasn't Reuben; no, it was Judah.

"My brothers, what gain will we make if we kill the boy and bury his body in the sand? Don't you see we have been favored? Let's sell him to these travelers and make some profit and get him off our hands at the same time." I could hear them agreeing with him, laughing with approval over this new development.

Finally they pulled me out. Where was Reuben? I looked around and couldn't see him. He'd promised he would come back for me.

I saw the foreigners hand money to my brothers, and then they pushed me toward them. *Reuben, where are you?* I kept calling for him in my mind, but I was too afraid to cry out.

The last thing Reuben said was not to say anything that would get them more angry than they already were. As the caravan took off, I looked back for a while. He wasn't coming, and I was alone.

***

It had been years since I last saw my brothers' faces. They looked old and tired. By this time I had children of my own. None of my brothers recognized me, and I didn't see how they could. I was more Egyptian than Canaanite. After I revealed myself to them, I tried to assure them not to be afraid—that it was God who allowed these things to happen to save our people from the famine. All were relieved, except Reuben.

He had separated himself from the group. I went over to him. His head was bowed. I could hear him crying, but this was different from the relief my brothers expressed. This was repentance.

"Reuben, it's all right."

"No it's not. I am your older brother. It was my duty to protect you. It was my responsibility, and I failed."

"No, you didn't. I believe God sent you away when I was in the pit in order for His purpose to be fulfilled. If you were there and stopped the caravan from taking me, then I wouldn't be in the position now to save my family.

"Yes, there were some difficult years, but as a good friend once said, the main thing is to stay true to who you are and no matter what, always keep your faith in God. He will help you navigate through life. And as for my brothers, I don't blame them, and I don't blame you. You shouldn't blame yourself either. As a matter of fact, Reuben, if you want to blame someone, blame God."

"How can I blame God?"

"Well, He allowed these things to happen for His purposes to be fulfilled. So my brother, there is nothing to forgive. Let's not waste any more time on the past. We have some living to do."

We held each other close, and then I could sense a bigger presence holding us. It was as if God Himself was putting His arms around us as we held each other. No matter how old we were, there was still time for reconciliation.

Then I heard Reuben pray, "Thank You, Lord, for bringing my brother back to me."

"Yes, thank You, Lord," I repeated.

And then through our tears, I heard the whispered words,

Part 3
Fathers

Have you ever been at a place in your life where you knew you were called to do something, but you just didn't know what it was? Like you were trying to find yourself, like Stephen?

Have you ever had the best sincere intentions, only to realize that you were sincerely wrong, like Simon the Zealot or Apollos?

Have you ever been in a situation where you were put to the test on God's Word and it seemed the next step was either do or die, like Naaman?

First John 2:14 says, "I write to you, dear children, because you know the Father. I write to you, *fathers*, because you know Him who is from the beginning. I write to you, young men, because you are strong, and the word of God lives in you, and you have overcome the evil one."

The following stories are about everyday men ranging from young to elderly and how they managed to get through difficult (and for some) death-defying circumstances and situations.

They found new faith, hope, and love, and as they went through their experiences and as you read their stories, it is my hope that you will see how they were able to answer one simple question:

Blessed

Then people brought little children to Jesus for him to place his hands on them and pray for them. But the disciples' rebuked them. Jesus said, "Let the little children come to me, and do not hinder them, for the kingdom of heaven belongs to such as these." When he had placed his hands on them, he went on from there. (Matthew 19:13–15)

"Nnnnnnnoooooooooo."

She was my goddaughter, but the girl was driving me crazy.

"No, no, no, no. I don't want to take a bath."

This must be the new word for the week. Anything we said, she said no.

"Elizabeth, come here, child."

"Noooo."

"Elizabeth, it's time for supper."

"Noooo."

"Elizabeth, it's time to go home."

"Noooo."

Mind you, if you thought you were losing your hearing, she confirmed you weren't. And if you thought you needed more exercise in your life—well, let's just say she was the one who made sure you got it. Her mother was on her own a lot as her husband was a fisherman. Most days he was out early and came in late. There were also the times when her mother, Margaret, had to work odd jobs to help make ends meet.

Martha and I were next-door neighbors of Elizabeth's. We were both retired and had grown attached to the young couple. We did have children of our own, but they were grown and lived in other townships. I guess as people go, we were near, dependable, but most of all we seemed to have the same kind of spirit. We believed the same kind of things, had similar interests, and loved the area we lived in.

"Lucas."

"Yes, dear."

"I have an idea. Why don't we take Elizabeth for a walk in the market? I need to get some things for the house, and it's a lovely day outside."

She looked at me and smiled. As women go, she was a beauty. Martha was a lady who grew graceful with age.

"Would you like to go to the market, Elizabeth?" she asked, smiling at the little girl.

"Yesssssss," Elizabeth said, smiling.

I shook my head in amazement. "The girl's a con artist," I cried out to Martha.

"What on earth are you talking about, Lucas? I asked Elizabeth if she would like to go to the market, and she said yes. What's wrong with that?"

I looked at the little girl and grumbled under my breath. Can you imagine? Everything I say I get a no, and here comes wonder woman, and with one request she gets a smiling yes.

"Well, you can carry her?" I said, feeling grumpy.

"Oh, Elizabeth, I think we have an old grouchy in the house," Martha said, smiling wide-eyed to the little girl. Elizabeth just giggled in reply.

The market was a busy place. Vendors lined the streets selling clothes, pots, fruits and vegetables, and jewelry.

"Lucas, can you hold on to Elizabeth? I'm just going to look at these materials."

"Wait, me hold her—why can't she go with you?"

"She's your goddaughter, for goodness' sake. You're like sixty plus, and she is just two. You mean to say you can't manage a little girl you have at least sixty years over?"

When she put it like that, it did sound ridiculous. But this child had another spirit in her.

"Now, Elizabeth, you be a nice little girl, and don't give Uncle Lucas any trouble, okay, sweetheart?"

"Yesss, auntie."

"Lucas."

"Yes, dear."

"Behave."

"Me—you're telling me!"

Martha shook her head with a little smile and left us standing.

"Okay then. Let's go and look at the pool." Elizabeth didn't say anything, so I took that to be a good sign.

I carried her and walked through the market till we reached the center. In the market center a little children's pool had been built, and on hot days the neighbors brought water from a nearby spring for children to wade their feet in.

I took off Elizabeth's slippers, and she was happy to go in. *Well, so far so good,* I thought.

After a short time, she found playmates, and they were playing and walking around together in the shallow water. The way children made friends seemed so easy. I got to thinking, if people could make friends so easily, then maybe the world would be a better place to live in.

"Okay, Elizabeth, it's time to go."

"Noooooooo."

Some of the mothers started to look at me with a look I thought said, "I wonder if he knows what he's doing."

"Elizabeth, baby, come now, honey. It's time to go and find Auntie."

"Noooooooo." The cry of resistance again.

Then I heard some mothers talking.

"Have you heard?"

"No, what?"

"Jesus, the healer; He's coming to our town."

"I heard He heals the sick and lame."

"Yes, and preaches the good news to the people," said another woman.

"I heard He's not like the priests or the Pharisees."

"I know; Jesus cares for people."

"I have an idea," another mother volunteered "Let's take our children to Him to be blessed. He loves little children."

"That's a wonderful idea."

One by one the women started to collect their children from the pool.

"Elizabeth."

"Noooooooo."

"Sorry, baby, but not today." I went in and picked her up. "You're going to get your blessing, even if I have to carry you there myself."

I gave her a stern look, and she calmed down and rested her head on my shoulder. After a short while we found Martha.

"Martha."

"Yes dear, is everything all right?"

"I just heard the Master, the one called Jesus, is coming to our town, and some of the women are carrying their children to be blessed."

"And …?"

"And I want my goddaughter to get her blessing."

"Well, since you're so keen on it, let's go."

We started off, and then I stopped.

"What's wrong?" Martha asked.

"I know receiving a blessing is a good thing, and I don't think Margaret would object, but don't you think we should ask her permission first?"

"Lucas, you're right; as her mother, she should have her say in this."

I looked at Elizabeth, and as she looked at me, it was as if she could tell we were in a predicament.

"We have to find her," I said. "Where did she say she would be working today?"

"I think she said she would be at the potter's house painting vases."

"Well then come on, woman, let's go."

"My, my Lucas; I swear if anyone saw the look on your face they would believe Elizabeth was your daughter."

I looked at Elizabeth and smiled, and then she smiled back.

"We're going to see Mommy. Yes!"

"Yes" she replied.

We found Margaret and told her the plan.

"Of course, of course she can get blessed."

"Can you take a break and come?" asked Martha.

"I wouldn't miss it for the world," she said, smiling.

When we got to the place where Jesus was sitting, there was a group of women ahead of us. We were just in time to hear His followers speaking to them.

"The Master is tired. We're sorry, ladies, but the Master can't spend time for little children. He has too much to do."

I could see the disappointment on their faces as they turned away.

"We're too late," said Margaret.

"Lucas."

"Yes, Martha."

"I'm sorry. I know you had your heart set on Elizabeth being blessed, but maybe it wasn't meant to be. Maybe another time; let's go home."

We were about to turn when I noticed Jesus talking to His followers.

"No wait, hold on a minute."

"What is it?" asked Martha.

"I don't know, but just hold on a minute."

Then we heard Jesus say, "Let the little children come to me, and do not hinder them, for the kingdom of heaven belongs to such as these."

"Here, Margaret, you take her. You go with her, Martha."

"Aren't you coming?" asked Margaret. "If it wasn't for you, we wouldn't be here."

"No, it's fine, you go. Go on, and I'll wait for you here."

She smiled and kissed me on the cheek; then she and Martha went and joined the women.

"And what's your name?" asked Jesus.

"'Isbeth," Elizabeth said, smiling happily.

"And who brought you here today, 'Isbeth'?" Jesus asked, smiling.

Then a funny thing happened. Elizabeth turned and looked and kept looking through the crowd. The women, realizing she was trying to look through them, stepped aside to give her a clear way.

Then she looked at me, pointed her finger, and said, "Unca Luuuu."

"Do you love your Unca Luuuu?" He asked.

"Yesssssss," she said, nodding her head.

Then He smiled, touched her head, and said, "Bless you, My child."

That evening as we got home, Elizabeth was sleeping on her mother's shoulder. We talked a bit about the day and were about to say our good-byes.

"You know, you did a good thing today," said Margaret. "I know you love this little girl; that's why we asked you both to be godparents." Then she looked at her sleeping daughter. "Elizabeth, you do have a father." Then she held my hand and said, "But …

Dinner for One!

So the king gave the order, and they brought Daniel and threw him into the lions' den. The king said to Daniel, "May your God, whom you serve continually, rescue you!" A stone was brought and placed over the mouth of the den, and the king sealed it with his own signet ring and with the rings of his nobles, so that Daniel's situation might not be changed. (Daniel 6:16–17)

Well I never expected that I would be judged for doing the right thing!

"Lord, how do you figure this one? Here am I, praying to You faithfully three times a day, even with my face facing the blessed Jerusalem. I'm doing my work to the best of my ability. I know You've gifted me with administrative skills, and my event planning and customer service are second to none. Lord, I understand You blessed me with a structured mind-set and strong key skills, especially when it came to organizing and planning. These things come from You and as the saying goes, "If you don't use it, you lose it." But I wonder why the other delegates resented discipline and order.

"They need it to have a good life, but they don't want the person You chose, Lord, to administer it."

"Hey you there, keep moving." The guard was prodding me with his spear.

"Young man, do you know that hurts?"

"Oh, I'm sorry, your Majesty. Is it too sharp? Don't worry, in a little while you won't feel a thing."

The two guards escorting me burst out in laughter.

The tunnel leading to the lion's den was really dark. I kept losing my balance, tripping on rocks and stones as I made my way to the open area.

"You know, Lord, maybe just maybe if I knew it was going to be like this I might have worked less. No, that would go against everything I believe in."

"Who is he talking to?"

"I think all that governing work has made him mad!"

"I heard some of the king's advisors say he prays to his God everyday without miss."

"Okay, so maybe he's praying to Him now?"

"Not sure how much help it will do. The lions haven't been fed for two days."

"With his frail frame, this won't take long."

And they laughed again.

"I'm glad you're enjoying yourselves at my expense."

"We have to, my lord. By the time you go in, you'll be gone." And they laughed again.

As we entered the den, I could tell it was approaching evening.

"Daniel." The call came from the mouth of the tunnel.

"My king," I replied.

"I have tried every possible way to get you out of this, but my advisors have trapped me in an iron-clad contract. The law states that no request should have been made to any other person or god for the next thirty days, and you broke that law."

"I know, my king, and I'm guilty. Your so-called advisors were not good enough to take my job from me by performance, so they chose deception to gain your favor."

"Daniel, please, tell me what to do. I—"

"My King, please, this is not of your doing. But I believe the God of Abraham, Isaac, and Jacob, the God of my fathers whom I pray to each day, will work in my favor. If I perish, I perish, but I cannot deny my God that which is due to His holy name. In His eyes there is only one true God. For me to abandon Him by making my requests be made known only to even you, my king—that, I just cannot do."

"Then may your God who you serve faithfully protect you."

"And you, my king, and you."

"Well, best of luck, my lord," chirped one of the guards as they retreated to the entrance we came through a few moments ago.

"Yes, see you … not." said the other, laughing as they walked away.

"Roarrrr."

The guards cut short their laughter and stepped up their pace as they disappeared into the darkness.

"Well, Lord, now it's just us."

"Roarrrr."

"I believe I was mistaken. It's us and them."

"Roarrrr."

Nobody had to tell me what that was. I took a deep breath through my nose. "Lord, is this it? I can do nothing, but You can do everything. Prepare my soul for Abraham's rest."

I settled into the thought of being eaten, but I hoped it would be swift. I could hear the rumble of a boulder being rolled against the entrance, then: *Boom.*

The sound not only sealed my fate, but I also felt my heart drop, as it were. I knew and trusted God in a way that was childlike, but I still had a feeling of being cut off from the outside world. I had to switch my vision from my physical eyes to my spiritual eyes, as it was those that I used in prayer as I directed my thoughts toward Jerusalem.

The den itself was circular in design and had one main passage that served as entrance and exit. I was led through to the east side of the den. I looked around and couldn't see anything. The evening shadows made most of the den dark. And then …

"Roarrrr."

"Okay, okay, okay, okay, okay."

Then I saw them; they looked bigger than expected. There was one lion and three lionesses. I froze. I thought I would run, but I didn't. I just stood there. I couldn't move a muscle.

The only movement I was conscious of was the in and out of my chest as I breathed.

"Hello, Daniel."

My head flicked in the direction of the salutation. "Hello? I thought I was the only person who was going to be fed to the lions; who are you?"

"They look tired, don't they? Locked in here so long … it's not right, you know."

"Excuse me! We're going to be eaten any minute and you feel sympathy for the diners?"

"Oh no, I'm sorry, Daniel; please allow me to clarify the situation. You are the one to be eaten at any minute, not me."

I looked at the man with amazement. Was he for real? Mind that, where did he appear from?

I didn't see another escort of soldiers following us down the tunnel. Was he here waiting to be eaten by the lions before I came?

"Lions are such brave creatures, don't you think?"

I was so engrossed by the man's calm demeanor, I didn't realize the male was brushing his mane against my leg. I felt the soft hair on the back of my hand but didn't realize he was actually there.

As for my newfound, mysterious friend, his hand was stroking one of the lioness's neck and back.

"They like that, you know."

"Okay …"

"Yes, they were made to be stroked and patted and live free. Not cooped up in a prison, like this place. Why don't you give it a try?"

I stroked the main of the male lion, and he gave out a low growl.

I couldn't take it any longer. I just had to ask.

"Excuse me but, who are you?"

"Oh … ummmm … you can just call me Angel."

"Angel?"

"Yes, that's right."

Angel kept stroking the lions. For a man who was second in command only to the king, I was catching on to the situation rather slowly.

"So, excuse me, Angel."

"Yes sir."

"What is happening here?"

"Well, Daniel, you really don't have a clue, do you?"

"I'm sorry, but no."

"You faithfully pray three times a day, right?"

"Right," I answered.

"So why should it surprise you when the God you pray to continuously answers your prayers and chooses to send one of His servants to help in a time of need?"

I was contemplating what he was saying.

"Hey, Daniel, I'm not saying you have to jump for joy or give a shout of praise or something, but you could show a bit more enthusiasm. I really don't get to travel to earth every day, you know. This is rather a special case."

"Er … um … thank you," I said weakly.

"No, no, my friend. Don't thank me. Thank God."

I bowed my head and felt so ashamed of myself. Here was God, providing away to keep me safe from harm, but I couldn't accept what He was doing. It was as if I was disappointed, like I should have been eaten by the lions.

"Forgive me, Lord, for doubting Your deliverance and love." I looked at the lions and smiled. "By the way … Angel?"

"Yes, my lord."

One thing with Angel, he seemed to be an upbeat kind of fellow.

"What actually happened to the lions anyway?"

"It's their mouths," he said, smiling.

"Their mouths?" I repeated with a curious look on my face.

"Yes. Their mouths are closed, shut tight. They couldn't open them even if they wanted to. They are so hungry. The Lord thought just to tell them not to eat you wouldn't be good enough as they haven't eaten in a while. He thought He would help them by removing temptation altogether so they wouldn't suffer tonight."

"Is that so?" I said, trying to sound as if I understood this level of working.

"Yes, you know, He's thoughtful like that. Always thinking of the little things; after all, if they can't taste the food, why would they want it?"

That actually made sense to me.

"So, what now?" I asked my newfound friend.

"Well, you can go to sleep if you like."

"Ahhh, I think I'll pass on that. I want to keep my eyes open."

"Scaredy cat."

"Yes, you are so right, and I'm not afraid to say it. Er, Angel."

"Yes, my lord, at your service," he said, smiling.

"I know you're enjoying yourself right now, but why is that lion looking at me like that?"

"I don't know; do you want me to ask him?"

I turned and looked at Angel with the most awkward look on my face.

"You speak lion?"

"Well, duh—what would I be doing here if I couldn't? You know, for someone who is such an intelligent being, you're really not that bright, are you?"

I should have felt insulted, but under the circumstances, I think I could accept that one.

"Well, what did he say?"

"Do you want to hear?" Angel said, smiling.

"Nooooooo … you can't do that, can you?" I said with a half unbelieving but half anticipating smile.

"Could be the chance of a lifetime," said Angel, smiling.

"Okay, let me in."

"He looks so thin," said the male.

"And I thought we were hungry," replied the female next to Angel.

"Angel."

"Yes."

"I can hear them; I can actually hear their words in my mind. God is a genius!"

"Yes, He is," said Angel confidently.

We talked for a while, and I finally laid down, using a lioness as my pillow.

"One day, Daniel," Angel started, "there's going to be a new heaven and a new earth, and a lion will lay down with a lamb. Old things will be past, and everything will be new."

When I looked at Angel's face, I could see the longing for that day in his eyes. And then he came back to the present. "Well, Daniel, it's been a pleasure, but the day is about to break and I must be on my way."

I didn't realize how the time had gone by. Here was I, talking with Angel and sitting in the company of lions.

"I won't forget this. Thank you. I really mean it."

"Daniel, you need to remember, you're not alone, you know. He not only hears your prayers, but your God responds to them too."

Then as suddenly as he appeared, he was gone.

"You do, Lord, don't You? You do respond to prayer."

Then I heard a still, small voice reply,

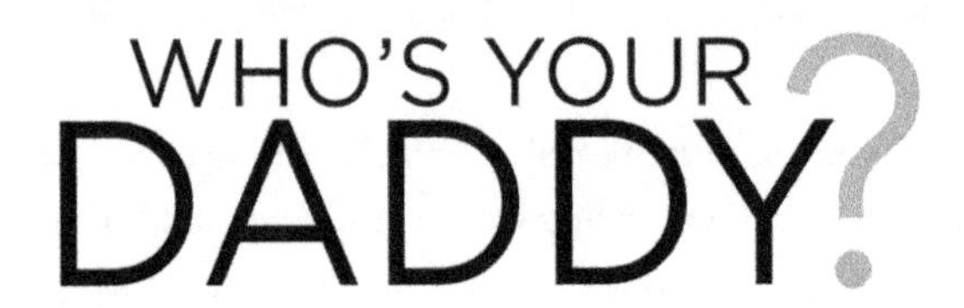

Finding My Purpose

Therefore, brethren, look ye out among you for seven men of honest report, full of the Holy Ghost and wisdom. ... And they chose Stephen, a man full of faith and of the Holy Ghost ... And when they had prayed, they laid their hands on them. (Acts 6:3-6)

Have you ever felt you were meant to do something major? I mean, I'm no superman, but when I see the elders teaching and preaching, I have a strong pull in my spirit to be doing something like that. I guess what the leaders have in common is that they all knew and walked with Jesus. I only heard of Him by secondhand account.

I studied the prophets and the law, and I was a diligent student, fascinated with the history of Israel. "Lord, I know I'm not the jealous type. Honest, I'm not jealous of anyone; I just have this strong feeling in my spirit that I was meant to do something more for You."

The problem is, I just can't put my finger on what I'm supposed to do.

"Hey, Stephen, have you heard?"

"Oh, hi there, Timon ... heard what?"

"Well, first of all, what's wrong with you? What's with the long face?"

"Sorry, I was just thinking, that's all."

"Oh, thinking about what to do in the church perhaps?"

I looked at Timon intently. He had a knack of reading situations quickly. "Look up there at the platform. We have so many leaders. How can they all preach at the same time?" I asked, not really looking for a reply.

"But preaching isn't the only thing they do, you know, Stephen; remember, they teach the Word, heal people, and cast out spirits, not to mention oversee the welfare of the whole church, which is growing in numbers daily, mind you."

"Yes, you're right. I'm sorry. I guess my vision has been a bit tunnel-like lately. There's a bigger picture I have to see, but it doesn't stop this feeling I have from going away."

"You know, Stephen, there is something I think you have forgotten in your thoughts."

"Yes, and what's that, my learned colleague?" I said with a relaxed smile.

"People here love you, you know. You are a good person. You're thoughtful, considerate, caring, and your zeal and love for the Lord are contagious."

"Contagious?" I repeated with a surprised expression on my face.

"Yes, contagious, as in infectious, catching, transmittable." Timon smiled as he continued. "Stephen, there is something—no, someone inside you that is evidently clear. I've seen it for myself. When you do speak about the Lord, I see a glow, as it were, radiate from your face. There is a strong passion in your voice when you speak about the love of God. And not only in your speech, brother—no, no—but in your actions too. Whatever you're looking for, give it time and it will come."

"Thank you, Timon. You're a good friend. I mean it."

There was a murmuring in the crowd and we could hear arguments between some of the women.

"Oh, that's what I came to ask you about."

"What's that?"

"Well, my learned friend," he said with a smirk on his face, "it seems with the increase of believers especially from Greece, their widows have brought a dispute to the leaders stating they have not been equally treated in the distribution of supplies in comparison to the Hebrew women."

"So what are you saying—there's discrimination among the fellowship?"

"I don't know for sure. We do have a history of not agreeing on certain terms, but the gospel is for all. I just don't know if we're ready to get past our past."

"So, is there a possible solution to all this? How can the church move forward if this controversy is alive among us? The most it will do is turn people away from the church and give others who already oppose us another reason to speak ill of us."

"Well, from what I understand, the leaders are in discussion now and will be addressing the whole congregation. Wait—as a matter of fact, I think it's going to happen now."

Just then we saw the leaders gather in unison at the main platform. They looked satisfied and in agreement with each other. I didn't see anyone trying to separate themselves, so that was a good sign, wasn't it?

Then James, Peter, and John, who were the main leaders of the church, addressed the congregation.[1]

"Brothers and sisters in Christ," John started, "it is not fitting that we should leave the Word of God to serve tables."

Peter continued, "Therefore, brethren, please look out from among you for seven men of honest report, full of the Holy Ghost and wisdom, who we can put in charge over this business."

Then James added, "But we will give ourselves continually to prayer and the ministry of the Word."

"Amen, Amen," came from the gathering of believers.

It looked like everyone was in agreement with the proposal put forward by the church leaders. During the next few days, believers both Jew and Greek came up to me asking if I would consider being nominated as one of the seven brethren. I was honored to be recognized, and to think that people in general held me in such high regard made me feel appreciated.

Timon was right. I was loved, and I thanked God for that acceptance. The issue I had was wondering if this was the thing I was looking for all along. Believing I had a bigger purpose to serve, was this it? To serve tables?

I was privileged and honored by the response of the people, but, "Lord … was this really what You had in store for me? My studying of the Scriptures, listening to the apostles teach, and commitment to prayer—was it all to serve in the distribution of food?

"Well, Lord, if that's what You called me to do, then by Your grace help me to do it to the best of my ability."

When the first day of the week came, we met again for service. The brethren called seven of us forward. Both Timon and I were chosen, along with five others. Besides Timon, I knew Phillip, but the others I had seen but not really been close to. We lined up in front of the congregation and kneeled down. The leaders prayed for God's guidance and wisdom as we were committed to the tasks ahead. I felt restless as the brethren prayed; I couldn't shake the feeling that there was more than this for me to do. Then I offered a prayer from my own heart.

1 Galatians 2:9

"Lord, if you can use anyone, please, Lord, use me. Take my heart and my life, and if it's even one time, make my life stand for You in such a way that it will cause a change in this world like no other."

The brethren laid their hands on us, and as I felt their hands on my head and shoulders, it was as if a new anointing of God's presence filled my very being. I was revived.

I felt set apart to do something new. Then a passage of the Psalms came to my mind almost as a confirmation of my consecration:

> Behold, how good and how pleasant it is for brethren to dwell together in unity! It is like the precious ointment upon the head that ran down upon the beard, even Aaron's beard that went down to the skirts of his garments. It is as the dew of Hermon, and as the dew that descended upon the mountains of Zion; for there the LORD commanded the blessing, even life for evermore.[2]

After this the Lord used me greatly to minister in the lives of people. God used me to heal and deliver people held by evil spirits and teach and preach the good news of the Savior.

"Do you want to start your own church?" asked Timon one day.

"No, my friend; it's just that the more I surrender myself to God's leading, the more He gives me gifts to use in His kingdom. It's not about me making a name for myself; it's about making myself available to be used at the right place in the right time."

"Well then, God be with you, my brother, but be careful. Unlike the church leaders who recognize your spirit, there are those who want to oppose the spirit that is in you."

"They won't be opposing me, Timon. Nothing I do is of my own making. They will be opposing the work of God."

True to Timon's word, a group of men in the synagogue formed themselves together with the purpose of disputing my claims that Jesus is the Christ. I wasn't afraid to take them on, but when they confronted me and couldn't find any loopholes in my arguments, they hired others to give false witnesses to the people, stating I had spoken evil against Moses and the customs he delivered to the people of Israel.

They brought me to the council, where the high priest asked me if the accusations were true. Then I felt it. It was as if at that moment, all my studies

2 Psalm 133

in the Scriptures, listening to the Word spoken by the leading brethren, and the completeness I felt in God's presence came together.

And beginning at Abraham, I opened my mouth and preached the history of our nation.

I preached of Abraham, Isaac, and Jacob. I preached of Jacob's children from who came the twelve tribes of Israel. I preached of Joseph and his sojourn in Egypt whereby God used his life to secure the lives of his brethren. I preached of the nation that grew in Egypt, their bondage by a new pharaoh, and their deliverance by our forefather Moses. I preached of the nation's backsliding in asking for a calf made of gold to worship when their faith in the one true God had turned. I preached of God's mercy and the tabernacle of witness and how the Lord gave Moses the instructions of how it should be built.

I preached of David, who returned the glory of Israel, and Solomon, who built the house of the Lord of which the prophet Isaiah said, "The heaven is my throne, and the earth is my footstool. Where is the house that ye build unto me? And where is the place of my rest?"[3]

I preached till I likened the leaders of the synagogue to the stiff-necked and uncircumcised in heart people who persecuted our forefathers the prophets. I told them that they were no better than those who resisted the Holy Spirit of God and put our Savior Jesus to death.

I preached till there was nothing else left to say. I preached it all.

Then a glorious thing happened. I looked up at the sky and saw a parting in the clouds and saw what I could only describe as glory. Jesus was standing on the right hand of God the Father. I didn't even realize I said what I saw out loud; I was so caught up in the splendor of it all.

Then the men ran to me and beat me. They even used their teeth to bite me, but my focus was on the Father and Son above. They threw me out of the city and continued to stone me, and all I could do was keep calling on the name of the Lord.

"Lord, thank You. Thank You I had the chance to stand for You. Thank You for being with me. Thank You."

I didn't think of praying for God to save my life; I prayed for Him to take it.

"Lord Jesus, receive my spirit."

As I knelt down and felt the stones hitting my body, I mustered the strength to let out one final cry: "Lord, lay not this sin to their charge."

3 Isaiah 66:1

Then, under my breath I prayed, "Lord, please receive me."

Then just as I closed my eyes I heard a soft voice say, "Welcome home, child, for after all is said and done,

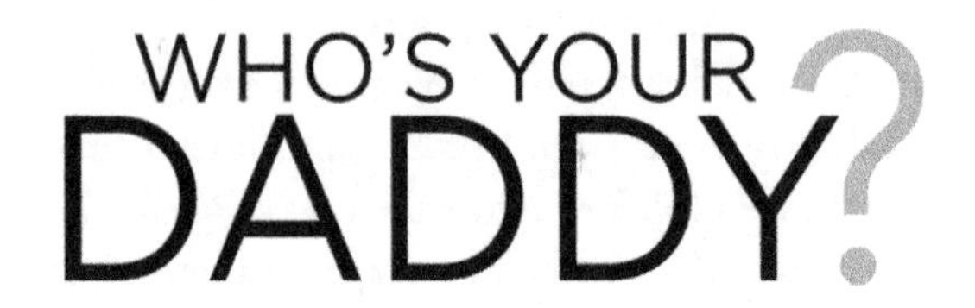

I'm the Dinner?

Now the LORD provided a huge fish to swallow Jonah, and Jonah was in the belly of the fish three days and three nights. (Jonah 1:17)

"Well isn't this something? Usually I eat fish for dinner, and here am I eaten by a fish." I guess this is the price you pay for disobedience. Oh, what a fool I am. How could I have been so simple? How on earth did I think I could run away from God? Really now, and what have I got to show for my troubles? A smelly bed, a dark room, and motion sickness.

If you've ever had the experience of being inside the belly of a fish, my friend, trust me, it's no ride in the park. I'm sitting on what I can only think of as a soft soaking carpet that wobbles from side to side. I keep losing my balance every second. There's no light, I can't see a thing, and the smell—ugh. Oh boy, I have to hold my nose and breathe through my mouth.

I feel seaweed around my arms and legs, and I'm cold, so cold. I would give anything if I could just stop moving, and now I can feel the fish going down deeper and deeper into the ocean. Wait; what's this? We've stopped. We're not exactly still, but it's like when a boat is anchored at sea, when there are no waves beating; just a gentle swaying as it were.

Why was I so headstrong? I was trying to keep myself so busy during the days trying to drown out the voice of the Lord. He told me what He wanted me to do: "Go to the great city of Nineveh and preach against it, because its wickedness has come up before me." But I still didn't want to listen.

The first time I heard God's call was when He told me to speak to King Jeroboam.[4] That was scary because King Jeroboam did some really bad stuff as king, following in the footsteps of his predecessor, another king called Jeroboam who was the son of Nebat.

4 2 Kings 14:23–29

Have you ever had to speak to someone who was in authority and point out to him that he had done something against the laws of God? My friend, it's not an easy thing to do, and I am not the boldest or bravest of men.

Why did God call me? What did I have? Does God have a way of choosing simple, everyday people to do great works? I mean, I was no Samson or Elijah; I was just a simple guy leading a simple life. And then one day I heard, "Jonah, Jonah."

"Oh, I know that voice—My Lord and my God."

"Jonah, I have a job for you. You are the one whom I have chosen. Arise, go to Nineveh, that great city, and cry out against it; for their wickedness has come up before Me."

"Lord, You see these people. Remember the last time You sent me to King Jeroboam? Lord, I was so frightened. He had a reputation for doing bad things to good people. Lord, it's a wonder I came back with my life still intact."

"Jonah, you do what I tell you to do. Obey My words, and heed My voice. The people will answer to Me, not you."

"Yes, Lord." And then He was gone.

What was God saying; was He serious? Didn't He realize the things we heard were taking place in Nineveh? If I went down there, it would be a suicide mission. Oh no, I'm not going down that route again. I'm out.

Where could I run to? I can't run away from God, but I won't know if I don't try. I have some friends in Tarshish I could stay with, but to get there I would have to take a ship. The nearest sailing port is Joppa. Let's see what I need to carry: some clothes, money for the fare … here's something my father Amittai gave me—a locket that his father gave him. We originally came from a small town called Gathhepher. The locket wasn't much, but it was mine and a way I had of remembering my father.

The easiest thing was getting to Joppa. No trouble there. Finding a ship and paying the fare, no trouble again. But when we got out to sea, I don't know where the storm came from. The captain said we should have a good sail before we left port, so as soon as the ship left the dock, I went down to the lower part of the hold and found a quiet place to sleep.

The captain and crew were arguing over whom or what caused the storm. It was unnatural. When they confronted me, I had no choice but to own up to it. It was one thing to put my life at risk running away from God, but to put the lives of these innocent men in danger? No, that was something I didn't want on my conscience.

"This whole thing is because of me. Throw me overboard and save yourselves. It's me my God wants, not you. If you do this, you will be saved. It's my fault you are all caught in this mess."

"Are you crazy, man? We would be committing murder. We may not be the most noble of men, but to sacrifice a life to save our own is not the code of conduct we live by."

"You are a good man, Captain, better than I, but look at your ship and your men. This vessel cannot take much more of a beating."

"No. Throw over the cargo, lads. Lighten the ship. Mr. Amish ..."

"Yes, Captain."

"Turn the ship starboard."[5]

"You men hold the rigging; we'll get through this. No man's life will be lost today," shouted the captain.

They fought with everything they had as I stood there watching, holding on to the side netting. "I'm telling you, Captain, pick me up and throw me into the sea. The storm will calm down once I'm gone. I know without the shadow of a doubt I'm the cause of this mess, and your lives will be saved."

Have you ever been in a situation where you knew that no matter what you did, the effort was pointless? You knew you were fighting a losing battle?

Watching these men fight with rigging and ropes, trying to tie things down, the harder they worked the stronger the sea became. Gales of wind slapped the sides of the ship, causing waves to rise and fall on the deck. These were grown men crying and shouting.

"Throw me in—now."

Then reluctantly they prayed, "Lord, we beg You, if we're wrong for doing this then in Your mercy, forgive us. Please don't judge us for this man's life. Don't let his blood be on our shoulders. You are God. We recognize that now. Oh God, do whatever pleases You."

About four men picked me up and held me for a moment, as if they were still hesitant if this was the right thing to do.

"After the next wave," the captain shouted.

---

5 Starboard is the right side of the ship perceived by facing the front of the vessel, which is called the bow.

The ship rocked sideways closer to the sea level as the water withdrew to collect itself for another onslaught.

"Now."

They threw me in. As I flew through the air, my heart was beating hard in my chest, trying to brace myself for contact.

Splash.

I hit the water hard. I wasn't a good swimmer, but I managed to wave my arms and kick my feet, working my way up to the surface. My head came up, and I managed to see the captain and crew looking at me from the port[6] side of the ship.

As I began to sink, I could see their images looking over. Then something amazing happened. The sky got bright and the water still.

It's as if the storm just stopped on command. I held my breath as I began to sink. For some strange reason, the thought that came to me was my father's locket. I had left it in my bag on the ship. I had lost everything, and for what? Because of my cowardly and disobedient heart. I was too afraid to believe God would give me the boldness to do the job He called me to do. I didn't believe He could use an everyday someone like me to bring an important message to a king; and on top of that, what would my father and grandfather say about my conduct. Running away from God? They would have been happy to know that the family line had an opportunity of being recognized in history for a life-changing, life-giving event but instead had to settle for the disappointment of knowing that I had boycotted God's command.

Then I felt him. I was sinking and slightly losing air when I felt a vacuum of water pull me in; then I felt a surface. Not a solid form but a soft, squishy surface. I rolled and rolled and then levelled off. It was dark, and I felt the water let out. Water still covered my hands as I crouched on my hands and knees, coughing, but I could breathe.

For three days I prayed like I never prayed before, calling on God for forgiveness and mercy, reminding Him of His greatness. I was asking Him to be merciful to me when I was merciless to the people of Nineveh. If I had thought of them and the judgement to face them, I would have played a different tune. But all I cared about was my own safety, and now not only did I put the lives of the Nineveh people at risk by not bringing God's message of salvation, but I also put the lives of the captain and his crew at risk too.

---

6 Port side is the left side of the ship facing the front of the vessel.

"Lord, forgive me for being so selfish."

The funny thing with learning a lesson is that you won't know if you've learned it until you're placed in a similar position again; then how you react in that situation will tell if you've learned it or not.

Was I a new person from this experience? Only time would tell.

"Lord, I'm sorry for putting You through so much trouble. If You give me another chance, I will do what You command, and in the process, Lord, if I can be used of You, help me to make in some way my father and grandfather proud of me."

Then, as if to confirm my prayers, I heard a still, small voice say, "Yes, My child, for after all …

I'm Too Tired to Listen

> And in a window sat a certain young man named Eutychus, who was sinking into a deep sleep. He was overcome by sleep; and as Paul continued speaking, he fell down from the third story and was taken up dead. (Acts 20:9)

You know one of the most difficult things with being in a Christian home is going to church when you're tired. Some people believe you must be at church every day of the week, and if you miss one service then, "You've turned your back on God, brother!"

Why can't people understand that I do love God; it's just that I get tired at times, and man, the worst thing to be is tired and in church. This night was to be a special night. Well, according to my parents anyway.

"Come on, Eutychus. Paul's time with us is short. If we don't get to church on time we won't even get a seat."

My mother, bless her soul, was always at my back insisting I make it to the fellowship times. But today was really a busy day.

"Yes, Mother," I said, trying to sound upbeat. The truth is, I've heard Paul speak and brother, I kid you not the man is *borrrrrrring*. To begin with, he speaks with a stutter, and that means he takes a good while to form a sentence. I couldn't understand it. There were church people who acted as if everything was fine. They looked intently into his mouth, taking in every word. Didn't they see how long he took? Or was it only me?

That night when we arrived at the church, the place was packed with people. It was Paul's last night, and everyone came out to hear him.

"Excuse me, excuse me, coming through," I said, respectfully trying to get through a group of people.

"Oh, Eutychus, I didn't expect to see you here!" It was one of the church leaders.

"Well … er … good evening, sir; I came with my parents, but we seem to have been separated in the crowd."

"Well then, I hope you enjoy the evening. We are all looking forward to hearing Paul share the Word one more time," he said with a smile.

I smiled back, out of respect rather than agreement. Everywhere I turned it was "Paul this" and "Paul that." Who was he, some kind of superman?

Then I felt a heavy hand grab me by the shoulder and pull me around.

"Eutychus." It was my dad. "Listen to me—I know you didn't want to come here, but if you try anything funny, you'll be cleaning sheep dung for the rest of the month. Do I make myself perfectly clear?"

"But Dad— the people, the crowd. It's not my fault I got lost; it just happened."

"Come on you," he said in a low, angry tone. "Your mother is over there waiting."

I don't know what it was with my dad. Nothing I did seemed to be good enough for him. Well, yes all right, I do admit, I was no angel. I took telling a few times before I actually did do some things, but I wasn't out on the streets at night making trouble or getting involved with the rebel groups against the Romans; that must count for something? But with Dad, he was always pushing me to do stuff I didn't want to do.

Clean the barn, help in the house, learn a trade—and then there was the worst thing he could say: read.

"Why did you have to handle him so harshly?" my mother said as Dad and I caught up with her. "And in front of our friends?"

"He's always disappearing, especially when we want him with us. I don't want him to get into any trouble." Dad sounded like he was trying to defend his actions rather than just talk to Mom.

"But husband, think for a moment. When does our son really get into any trouble? I know you want what's best for him and you are trying to steer him in the right path, but we both should be careful that we're not trying too hard to steer him when he is following the right path in his own way."

Dad looked on in silence; you could tell he was in thought mode by how he looked at her.

Was this a mother thing? How she could read between the lines of my father and me? I don't know how, but it worked.

"Eutychus."

"Yes, Dad."

"I think I saw Marcus and some of your friends over the far corner. Why don't you go say hello? Your mother and I will be over on the east side. We'll meet up at the front door later."

I looked at him, a bit surprised, but I felt for the first in a long time relaxed around him. I was going to say something, but the words stopped in my mouth. "Ummm thanks, Dad. I'll see you later." I smiled, kissed Mom on the cheek, and left.

Come to think of it, I've never seen Dad show affection to Mom outside our home. I wonder if he felt embarrassed to show affection in public. As I turned to leave, I heard my Mother say to him, "Now that wasn't so hard, was it?"

"Hey, Eutychus, I thought you weren't coming." It was Marcus. He and I were good friends. Both of us were similar in our views and the things we liked. But we did have a slight competitive streak that got out of hand once in a while.

"Yeah, well, I wasn't, but Mom and Dad insisted."

"Likewise. I heard Paul is a strong disciple for the Lord, so I'm hoping to hear some good stories of his travels."

"Have you ever seen Paul before?" I asked, really wondering if we were talking about the same person.

"No, no. But from the stories I've heard, he must be a great man. You know like one of the prophets, like Samson or Elijah."

"Really? Tell me more," I said, smiling, I didn't mean to be sarcastic, it was just one of those moments.

"Well, I just heard some people talking, and they say he's been through Macedonia, Greece, and back through Macedonia and parts of Asia before coming here to Troas. A guy who does that much traveling and speaking must have some good adventure stories to tell."

"*Shhhhhhh*," I interrupted. "They're bringing him in."

When Paul came out, led by the church leaders, everyone stood.

"Eutychus, can you see him? I can't see a thing with so many people, and on top of that it's hard to breathe. It's like someone's taking up all the air."

"For once I can say amen to that, brother. I need a new location."

From our seat the best we could see was the top of Paul's head. My friend was more disappointed than I was.

"I thought he was a bigger man—like your dad."

"How do you figure that?" I was curious to find out.

"Well no one in their right mind would mess with your dad. Even a Roman would think twice. And this guy, I can't see him because he's so bent, and I can't hear him clearly because he stutters."

It's funny, you can be with a person every day and not see them for the things they have, and it would take an outsider, in this case my friend, to point out that my dad was a physically well-built man. Why didn't I see that before? At that moment a bit of pride swept inside me.

It was nice.

"You know what?"

"No, what?" replied Marcus quickly, looking very pleased with himself.

"I think I need to find another vantage point."

"E … the place is packed. Where do you think you're going to find another seat?"

"What did the minister say last week in devotions? When you pray and don't see an answer around you, then look up."

"Yes, as in look up to the hills from where comes our help, our help comes from the Lord. What are you getting at?"

I could sense the cedar wood burning in his brain. Tilting my head, my eyes caught the beams supporting the roof and followed them to a window. "No, no, no, no, no, no, no, no, no, my brother." Then he tapped my head. "Hello, is anyone awake up there? You're thinking like a headless chicken."

I scowled at him.

"Don't look at me like that. That place is high. What if you drop off?"

"I won't drop off; that only happens to foolish people."

Then Marcus looked at me intently. "You know the evil thing about this?"

"What?" I said impatiently.

"Your parents are going to have a field day with me. It's gonna be, 'Marcus, how could you let this happen. You're supposed to be the sensible one and now our son is dead, and it's all your fault.' Not to mention what my parents are going to say."

"Oh, stop being so melodramatic," I snapped.

He looked at me with his lips pressed tight, squinting the corners of his eyes. He wasn't pleased, but that didn't stop me. I wanted a better seat.

The building we used for service was built with three balconies that went around the walls. On each side of the building, there were steps leading from the ground floor to the first, second and third levels.

People were standing in the corridors and on the stairways.

Paul was on a platform in the center of the hall. It wasn't that he was short in any way; it was just the sheer company of people. The place felt hot and miserable.

After reaching the second floor, I could see my parents sitting together, leaning forward to hear Paul speak. I looked at Dad and smiled.

What Marcus said about "not to be messed with" came back to me. But at the same time, I didn't want him to see me up here either; he would really blow his top.

Okay on the third level; now, how was I going to reach the roof beam? It was about five feet above my head. Then I noticed the edge of a bench that had a small vacant space.

Facing the edge of the bench, which was about a foot wide, I put my left foot up on the edge of the seat. The man sitting there was so into the sermon he wasn't paying attention to what I was doing. Then I pushed down on my left leg and sprang up. I reached for the beam with both hands and held on. I swung for a brief moment, then pulled my body up till my arms were straight above the beam with my hands flat on the top, then I slowly pulled my left leg over the beam to sit facing the wall.

I held the beam with both hands and leaned slightly forward. Body stiff, I pushed off the beam then pulled up both legs so my knees and toes were on the beam too.

Like a cat I moved on all fours closer to the wall. When I got to the wall I stood up slowly, balancing myself and reached for the open widow. Holding on to the windowsill, I pulled up again and with a quick twist of the hips sat on the windowsill, leaning my left shoulder on the frame. Mission accomplished. I started to relax and adjust my breathing and weight to the height.

I saw Marcus looking up at me in disbelief, holding his head with his hands shaking from side to side. I smiled and gave him a small wave. I had the best seat in the house.

Paul was going on and on. What he spoke of was good, but the heat in the room was rising to the ceiling and coupled with that was the fact that I was already tired before I came to the meeting. I fought to keep my eyes awake. I felt myself jerk a few times but pulled myself up when I felt my balance sliding from one side to the next. Then I couldn't hold it any longer.

I closed my eyes and felt my breathing get deeper and deeper. In an unconscious way, I tried to hold on to the window frame. Thinking I was back in bed at home, I turned over to pull the cover over me and slowly rolled off the windowsill.

I was falling. I wondered, *Am I dreaming or is this real?* My eyes opened slightly, but I couldn't see anything.

"Eutychus."

It was my mother's voice. "Yes, Mother?" I answered, wondering if it was morning already.

"Eutychus."

She cried again, shaking my senses more clearly, then looking down I saw the ground approaching fast. My heart raced.

"Oh God," I cried, breathing faster and faster. Then turning quickly to see him, I shouted out, "Dad."

I squeezed my eyes shut, then, nothing. When I came around Paul was leaning over me.

"Don't be afraid."

"Why should I be afraid?"

"You took quite a fall," he said, smiling.

Then he turned to the crowd. "The boy will be just fine," he called out.

"Praise God, praise God," someone cried.

"Eutychus." It was Dad. "Are you all right, son?"

"Yes, Dad," I said weakly. "Where's Mother?"

"I'm right here."

"Mom."

"I'm here, son." Then I saw her beside him.

We all held each other tight for a good while. It was the closest we'd been as a family in as long as I could remember. They helped me up, and you could see the amazement and the buzz going on among the church members.

"Do you remember anything?" said Dad.

"I remember calling you. I thought you were the only person strong enough to stop me from falling."

"Well, that's quite a bit of faith you have in me there, son," he said with a smile.

"I'm sorry, Dad. I should have listened. I'm sorry for causing you trouble."

"Don't worry. The most important thing is that you're all right. And besides, something like this doesn't happen every day."

That night, I laid down in my bed looking at the stars through my window. I was dead. Literally dead for a while today; what was I thinking? Making fun of Paul when he brought me back to life—finding a new respect for my dad, only to realize he didn't have life and death in his hands.

"Lord, thank You for both Paul and my dad. My parents gave my life at birth, Paul gave me life today, but You are the real giver of life. Help me to be a better son and servant for You. I need You."

And then in the quietness of the night, like a whisper or a breeze, I heard the reply:

My Past, My Present, My Future

> One of those days Jesus went out to a mountainside to pray, and spent the night praying to God. When morning came, he called his disciples to him and chose twelve of them, whom he also designated apostles: Simon (whom he named Peter), his brother Andrew, James, John, Philip, Bartholomew, Matthew, Thomas, James son of Alphaeus, *Simon who was called the Zealot*, Judas son of James, and Judas Iscariot, who became a traitor. (Luke 6:12–16)

"Come on Simon, come on, or you'll miss the beginning."

"You know, I'm right behind you," I said in a calm voice.

"Through here."

The streets of the city were small and had many pathways and alleys.

Not much thought had gone into house planning. It was just "build beside your neighbor." Because of this, there weren't many big houses that could hold a large number of people.

"What's this guy's name again?" I asked my friend.

"Justus," Matthias replied.

"His words, like yours, ring true of what's happening to our people. Come on, Simon. You said you were looking for fellow zealots like yourself; this man is one of us."

We entered an inn, and everything looked quiet. There were few tables and chairs, and the innkeeper was serving wine to someone in front of him.

"Follow me," said Matthias.

We turned and followed the stairs up to the second floor, and then he jumped up and pulled down a ladder that was attached to the ceiling. We climbed up and knocked three times on the latch door. A man opened it, and as we climbed in, we were just in time to hear Justus begin.

"My brothers, how long will we let these Romans rule over us? They tax our going out and our coming in. Who are they to tell a man when to sleep and when to rise?"

"Yes, yes," came a chorus of cries from the men who gathered. I could count at least fifty in the loft listening with agreement.

"Our so-called religious leaders say one day a Savior will rise again in the nation of Israel like our beloved King David. And when that day comes, he will free us from the bondage of our captors. Instead of us paying taxes to them, they will be paying taxes to us."

Justus continued, and I could tell he was growing in confidence.

"Brothers, we need arms, swords, and spears. We need to train to fight the Romans and drive them from our borders."

"But when will that day be?" someone shouted from the crowd.

"Remember Theudas?"[7] another man asked. "He thought himself to be the forerunner of the Deliver, and about four hundred men gathered to his side. And what happened to him? He was killed and his following scattered. Nothing came out of his rise for resistance."

"Yes, and what of Judas of Galilee?"[8] another man called out. "For those of us who remember, in the days of the taxing he convinced a lot of people to follow him, and when he suffered the same fate, what became of his following? Scattered … like dust in the wind."

Justus tried to gain back the crowd. "Brothers, brothers we can—"

"Soldiers, soldiers are coming. Run, everyone, run," the cry came out.

People were trying to get down the stairs. Others jumped through windows.

Matthias and I made our way to the platform where Justus was speaking and noticed another latch door in the roof.

"Up there." I pointed. "Come on," I called to Justus, and the three of us started climbing the wall. Just before the soldiers burst into the room, we pushed open the ceiling door and made our way to the roof.

"Well brothers … thank you and take care of yourselves," said Justus. "We stand a better chance of not being caught if we split up."

We nodded, and he took off.

"Where you go I go," Matthias said, smiling.

---

7 Acts 5:36
8 Acts 5:37

I shook my head. "Why is it you're always good at getting us into trouble and I'm the one good at getting us out?"

We made our way down the side of the roof and jumped from there on to the flat roof of a house close by.

"Up there … on the roof," a soldier shouted from the ground. "Follow them. They must be the leaders."

All I could feel was my feet running on the roofs of the houses as we ran and jumped from rooftop to rooftop. After we cleared the third roof, I jumped first and landed, rolling as I hit the surface.

Matthias jumped but fell short.

"Simon," he called out as he landed just on the wall, his hands clenching the edge of the roof. The soldiers were still following us on the ground.

I grabbed his hands just when they passed.

"Quiet" I told him. "We're in the shadows, and they may not see us."

The moonlight shone on the street, but we were covered by the shadows of the taller building.

"Do you see them?" a soldier asked.

"I think we lost them," another answered. "The commander is not going to like this. He wants the leader. He's not interested in the followers."

Matthias was shaking, but I kept my head down and held him tight.

Finally they gave up.

"Let's go—it's too dark," the first soldier said, and then they left.

I pulled him up, and we headed home. "That was close. Thank you, brother."

"Next time, Matthias, find your own window." We laughed and went our separate ways.

A couple days passed, and I didn't see Matthias again. I wondered which leader he was following now. Then as soon as I thought about him, he turned up at my door.

"Simon, I've found him."

"Found who, Justus?"

"No the Messiah, the Deliver, the one Justus spoke of."

"Is that where you've been lately? Following this Savior of the people," I said in a sarcastic way.

"Okay, I understand that after our last episode. But believe me, brother, He says things no one else has said and does things no one else does. I've seen Him heal people."

"Heal people? Only a prophet from God would have the power to heal people."

"But I've seen it with my own eyes, brother. There was a man full of leprosy who fell on his face begging the Master to heal him, and the Master reached out his hand and touched him and said, 'I will, be thou clean,' and he was clean, brother, from the crown of his head to the soles of his feet.[9] He's real, brother. He's real."

I'm not sure what grabbed me with Matthias; was it the possibility that the Scriptures were finally being fulfilled and the Savior of Israel had come? Or was it just his passion?

This was not the friend who pulled me to the zealot meeting. No, there was a change in this man. It was as if he had found a new life and I was becoming jealous of it.

"Okay, show me, Matthias. Where can I find this Savior?"

For the next few days we followed Jesus. His words were like no other. The things He spoke were what I thought of—deliverance and a new kingdom for the people of God. But it wasn't an earthly kingdom like what the nation had under David. Jesus spoke of a heavenly kingdom. It sounded good, but it's not what I wanted. I had a struggle inside.

Then one day Jesus disappeared. He went up to a mountain to pray. He stayed all night, but unlike with the other leaders, no soldiers came to disburse the people and no one left.

When He came back in the morning, He started to choose people to be His closest disciples. Apostles, He called them. Then to my amazement, He called me.

I couldn't handle it; I had to talk with Him.

"Jesus, Master, You called me."

"Yes, Simon, I did. Do you have a question?"

"Lord, I'm listening to You, but I don't understand how Your words can be so different from what I've learned. Look at all these people; how can one man gain the attention of so many? If the people understood what I believed, that

---

9 Luke 5:12

Israel must fight for their freedom from the Romans, could You imagine the army we would have?"

"Yes, Simon, you're right. If the people believed what you have been taught, then you would have an army. But do you think our Father needs an army to deliver His people? How many battles did our Father fight for His people in the Scriptures, and did they learn?"

I considered what Jesus said. It was true. How many fights did the Lord go before His people, and to what end? The people still turned their backs on Him. And now, every resistance was destroyed; it was as if I kept placing my faith in a man instead of the God of our people.

"Jesus, Master, will You teach me how to be an apostle and help me turn from my past to a new future?"

And then Jesus said with a comforting smile, "Simon, follow Me as I follow My Father, and let me show you truly …

Seven Times! Really?

Then went he down, and dipped himself seven times in Jordan, according to the saying of the man of God: and his flesh came again like unto the flesh of a little child, and he was clean. (2 Kings 5:14)

Well aren't I a sight for sore eyes. Here am I, commander of the armies for the king of Aram, great and honorable, a mighty warrior and leader standing here in the middle of the Jordan River. Why did I listen to that little Jewish girl? She is a sweet little thing and my wife did take a keen fondness to her, but to stake my reputation on her advice? But come to think of it, no one else was coming forward with any bright ideas.

This leprosy was killing me slowly; this was one thing I couldn't fight—not with a weapon or medicine or even magic. This was the only battle I didn't have an answer for.

"Are you all right, my lord?" It was my head servant, Amos.

"Do I look all right to you?" I snapped. "Why here? Why this place?"

"I'm sorry, my lord. I don't know. All I know is we all want to see you well, and if this is all it takes …" He shrugged his shoulders.

I looked around at the company of soldiers and servants. They all, along with the captains, had worried looks on their faces. "*Well*", I thought to myself, "*only you can make the decision to go through with this. It's either obey the prophet or leave.*" I was standing at waist high in the river. The water was mucky and dark, not like the clean waters of Damascus.

Dip One

As I closed my eyes and went down, the water was cold. I made sure to cover myself completely and felt my whole body temperature drop to the same level as the water. I held my breath, thinking possibly if I did one long dip then I would be healed. I held my breath for a few minutes; then when I couldn't hold it any longer, I came up with a rush, splashing the water with my arms.

"Am I headed? Am I whole?" I shouted to the guards standing on the riverbank. They looked at me with no answer. Everyone looked uncomfortable, and some held their heads down.

"No, my lord," said Amos. He couldn't even look at me when he spoke.

"What do you mean no?"

"Look for yourself, my lord."

"What?" I shouted. Amos pressed his lips into a slight smile and gently shook his head. I think the men were more disappointed than I was. I looked at my hands and arms, and I was angry. I was a military leader. I was a strong man. I was ... I was ... proud. That was it, wasn't it? My pride was hurting more than the pain the leprosy caused.

Dip Two

I went down again. Well, holding one long breath for healing didn't work. Under water I began to think about what my head servant said when I first received the instruction to dip seven times. I was so angry. "My father." He wasn't my son, so why did he call me father?

***

I called him father because as much as he was commander of the guard, he treated me and all the servants in his household well. We just wanted him to be healed. Sometimes when you meet someone who takes you in and cares for you, you just want to see him or her enjoy life. That's why I had to take the risk and speak to him even though he was so angry.

"My father." Naaman turned and looked at me as if he wanted to kill me, but I knew his anger wasn't directed at me. It was his pride that was hurt, but I couldn't stand by and let his pride get in the way of this opportunity for healing.

"If the prophet had asked you to do something great, wouldn't you have done it? How much more, then, when all he says to you is, 'Wash and be clean'?"

"Well, you do have a point, but it doesn't mean I have to like it."

"Yes, my lord, but everyone here"—I gestured to the men—"just wants to see you well again."

***

This time I started to rub my arms and body. Maybe if I scrubbed myself then I'd get clean.

I rubbed and rubbed, but all I did was feel more pain on my skin. I came up, and after the water had run off my face, I looked at my body.

"Arrrrrrrrrrrrr," I shouted. I closed my eyes and tried to calm down and breathe slowly.

Dip Three

I went down again. Maybe if I thought of something good. I started to think about my wife and the day we met. I was at the king's wedding. I was a captain at the time. At the reception I saw this lovely lady in a red, flowing dress. She was captivating and had the loveliest smile.

I learned later that it was my smile that caught her eye. It seemed she had a thing for nice teeth.

We courted for a while, and when the time was right, I asked her father for her hand in marriage. I pictured her face. "*What was that?*" I jumped up out of the water and shook my body. I calmed down and realized it was just a fish that was passing by and rubbed my back. I looked at my body; no change. It didn't even look like I was starting to heal. Well, thinking about my wife didn't do it. What was the prophet thinking?

Dip Four

And here we go again. I wondered if four would be the lucky number. *"What did four signify? Well, four divided the times of the day: morning, noon, evening, and midnight. It separated the seasons of the year: spring, summer, autumn, and winter.*

"But what had that got to do with healing? What else? North, east, south, and west, the four regions of the earth maybe, and there are the elements: earth, air, fire, and water." I knew I was fishing for something that wasn't there. The prophet said seven, not four.

But I guess I was trying to find a loophole—a way to get out of going the distance. If I went the distance, then the prophet would have won. It would mean that I, as strong and mighty as I was, had obeyed the words of a prophet of a nation I had defeated.

"Oh stop—come on and stop this nonsense." What did I want? Wasn't it to be healed? So if the prophet's words would make that happen, then what was I arguing about? I rose up out of the water, but this time I had no expectation that I would be healed.

"My lord."

"Yes, Amos."

"Your servant was wondering … when you are made whole, will you and my lady be taking a leave of absence?" Amos smiled.

"I'll consider it, but I'm sure my lady would be most pleased." One thing with Amos—he took chances with my patience. When I looked at my men, they were looking at me encouragingly. They wanted the same result as I.

Dip Five

I went down again. And as I did I thought about the prophet. He didn't even come out to see me when I came to his home. He sent out his servant. "*What was that man's name again? Oh yes, Gehazi; five times for five days?*

"Oh, Naaman, give it up. It's not about trying to figure out on which number the healing is going to happen." Every time I looked at myself, there was no change. "*What was this really about? I went to the prophet for help. He gave me an instruction. Now, he was a prophet for a reason. God spoke to the prophet, and the prophet spoke to His people.*

"Wait a minute; did that mean when I spoke to the prophet, the God of Israel was speaking back to me through him? Then the answer the prophet gave me about bathing in the river seven times didn't come from him—it came from his God.

"If that's the case, then what does God want from all this?"

"Obedience."

I opened my eyes and looked around. There was no one else in the water, so where did that voice come from? I stood up.

"Did you hear it?" I called to Amos.

"Hear what, sir?" he called back.

I hesitated to answer. It was enough that I had leprosy and now to add to that insanity.

What would my men think if I told them I was hearing voices? But I was sure it was a voice.

It sounded so clear.

"Nothing, don't worry about it."

Amos looked on with a half-unsure smile. "*I should distract the men before they think I'm going crazy*", I thought to myself.

"Well, just two more to go."

"Yes, my lord," they answered in unison.

"When we leave this place, we'll be sure to pay a visit to the prophet and show him how we reward those who honor our king's wishes."

"Arrrrrrr," the soldiers replied.

Dip Six

I guess they knew I was just trying to put on a brave face, but they were too loyal to expose it. I went down again. "*Why the number seven?*" That's it—I'd think of the things that had seven.

"Well, there was the most obvious, seven days in a week, but what has that got to do with healing? Wait; hold on a minute. What did that little Israelite girl say one time?

"That the God of their people made the earth in six days and on the seventh day He rested. Was seven the day of the Israelite God? It was—now I remembered. It was the day they put aside to give thanks and worship their God. Day seven, number seven, seven times in the Jordan River.

"Don't you get it, Naaman? The lesson is about recognizing who God is. The voice, the one that talked to me, it was Him. I know it—I just know it. Yes, the Jordan River was a dirty place, but it was the river of the Israelite people. It was the place of blessing, and if I wanted mine, I was at the right place at the right time.

"Come on, man, let's not waste any more time. God didn't want me to try to figure out why the number and why the river. It should have been enough to know that He ordered it. And now I had a choice. I could either accept and believe that my healing was near because God said so or walk away in pride." I came up out of the river smiling. When I looked at my body, there was still no change, but it didn't matter. I looked at the men and everyone who was watching.

I smiled, nodded my head, and went down.

Dip Seven

As I went down, I found my praise.

"Lord, I'm sorry for being so full of pride. I understand that You are in control

of all things. It was You who gave us the victory. I was under Your command and not my own. I realize, Lord that you rule in the affairs and hearts of men, and no man should think he is all powerful or equal or greater than You, almighty God.

"Lord, thank You for Your healing power. I believe I am healed not because there is some magic in the water and not because of who gave the command but because I believe You are a rewarder of them who obey Your Holy Word.

"And now, my God, make me clean, make me whole, not because I ask You, Lord—far from it. I ask you to heal me Lord—not for my sake, or for the sake of my family or the sake of my men and the king whom I serve, but for Your glory, Lord, that You will be glorified in this place."

I stood up out of the water, and as I rose, I heard a great cheer come from the riverbank. I let the water run off my head and down my face before opening my eyes. I looked down and saw my hands and body had skin as clean as a newborn baby. The men cheered again, and I looked at Amos. He was laughing and crying with relief and happiness.

"Men and brethren; be it known today, there is no other God like the God of Israel," I shouted. Cheers rang from the sides of the river.

"Thank You, Lord," I whispered.

Then the voice I heard before came back and replied, "You're welcome, my boy, for after all is said and done …

Speak the Word

When Jesus had entered Capernaum, a centurion came to him, asking for help. "Lord," he said, "my servant lies at home paralyzed, suffering terribly." (Matthew 8:5–6)

The war was bitter and tough. I had seen enough bloodshed to last a lifetime. We came back to Capernaum to the greeting of the people, Romans and Jews alike. The Romans liked the idea of us being the force to be reckoned with, and the Jews liked the protection we gave.

Riding through some villages and towns, I heard talk of a man people say was a prophet. He was healing the sick, giving sight to the blind, and giving hope to people of a better way of life. For all the fighting I'd been called on to do, I was growing weary of the life I had and longed for some of that peace people say this man spoke of.

"Sir, the men are all accounted for and ready for discharge," my captain reported.

"Carry on, Captain. Dismiss the men; we're all due a well-deserved rest."

A servant came and took my horse to the barns. As I walked through the city center to my home, I could see the synagogue and other places I had helped the Jews restore.

I had some of the Hebrew Scriptures in my possession and often read of the victories the children of Israel had in the past. What fascinated me more than anything else as a centurion was how the God of the Jews went before them in battle.

I did come across some wars they lost, but it was my understanding that those were due to their own disobedience. But the wars they won and the way they won the battles were nothing less than miraculous.

For example, in the book of Exodus when the children of Israel fought against the Amalekites, God told Moses that the battle was theirs so long as his arms were raised. But as soon as he got weary, the army started to lose the fight. Then two of his men went up and held up each arm until the battle was won.

Or the time in Joshua when the Lord told the army to march around Jericho one time a day for six days and then on the seventh day march around seven times and give a shout. To think, it was the shout of the people that brought down the walls of Jericho. If I had that much power on my side, I wouldn't have to fight so much.

But some of the Lord's ways are really unorthodox. I remember reading in the book of Judges ; the God of Israel spoke to Gideon and told him he had too many people for God to bring the Midianites into his hand. The Lord knew Israel might boast that they won the battle themselves, so their God had Gideon reduce the army to three hundred. What's interesting is their God still went before them and sent the Midianites into a panic, and they started to attack their own men.

One thing that did stand out in that story is the selection process the God of Israel gave them. Now Roman soldiers have a height requirement. Physical body strength is important to carry a shield and sword and hold a line against an approaching enemy. It's not a game of the weakest link.

But with Gideon, his God told him the people were too many. I would be honored to lead an army of thirty-two thousand men, but for God this was too many. Then the first thing He commanded was to send away all who were afraid, and twenty-two thousand deserted. Now ten thousand soldiers weren't great, but it was a reasonable number to start a battle with, but it was still too many for God.

And their God said what? Take the men down to the river, and anyone who laps the water in their hands, choose them, but anyone who bows their head to the river to drink, send them home. Now really, what kind of selection process was that? But I guess it worked because they won.

I think as a soldier and a centurion, studying the battles in the Scriptures gave me a better appreciation of the working of the Jewish God. For this reason I tried to follow their ways as best I could. I built places of worship and tried my best to show the people goodwill and favor. I believed that by showing the people favor, I was pleasing the God of the Jews, and hopefully their God would be my God one day, if I continued to serve.

As I arrived home, I was greeted with bad news. Every time I came home after a battle, I was welcomed by my head servant, Matthew. Matthew was a Jew. He was loyal and trustworthy. When I read the Scriptures, we talked sometimes about the meanings and lessons one could learn from them. I could tell by the looks on the other servants' faces that something was very wrong.

"Suzanna."

"Yes, my lord."

"What is going on? Where is Matthew? Why isn't he here? And why do all the servants look as if someone just died?"

"My lord, it's Matthew. Sir, a few days ago he caught a terrible illness, and we don't know what to do."

"Did you call for a doctor?"

"Yes sir, we did." She was trembling as she spoke.

"And? Well, speak up, woman," I shouted.

She cried even more.

"Suzanna, Suzanna, I'm sorry. I didn't mean to shout at you like that. Please, let's calm down a bit, and you tell me what's happened."

I smiled reassuringly, and she dried her face, took a deep breath, and continued.

"Well, my lord. We sent for the doctor, and he came yesterday. He said Matthew had caught an infection, possibly from someone in the marketplace. You know Matthew has a good heart, my lord. We know him to sometimes give money to poor or feeble folk. The doctor thinks he may have gotten too close to an infected soul, and now he has caught the disease himself."

I remained quiet as I wanted to give her as much time as she needed.

"It's been terrible, my lord. His arms and legs just keep on shaking without control. He will sleep for a while, but as soon as he wakes up, he shakes uncontrollably again."

She started crying again.

"How much time does he have?"

"The doctor gave him another week, maybe two at the most. He says there's nothing he can do."

I went down the corridor leading to the servants' quarters and down a stairway to his room.

A few servants were standing outside his door. Matthew was a good man. He ran my house well and treated everyone with respect. The atmosphere in the home was always pleasant as his order made people feel accepted, informed, and supported. The older staff he talked to like they were brothers and sisters and the younger as if they were his nieces and nephews.

I pushed the door and went in.

"Sir, you're safe. Welcome home," he said with a smile. His body kept shaking.

"Matthew." I wasn't sure what to say.

"Sir, I will be all right. My God will welcome me into Abraham's rest."

"But what if we're not ready to see you go?"

"Death is a part of life, sir; you know that more than anyone."

"I've seen so much death on the battlefield; I've gotten sick of death. I just didn't think of it coming into my home."

"Is that why you do the things you do, sir? I mean the building of the synagogue, the rebuilding of people's homes, not to mention the offerings you give on the Sabbath."

"I'm just trying to do my part—you know that."

"What I see is a man who is trying to buy peace for his soul. My lord, while the people appreciate these things, that you honor our faith and our God, our God doesn't want things first."

"Is that so? Then what does He want first?" I questioned.

"I believe you know the answer to that too, my lord. We have studied the battles long enough to know our God wants you to give Him your heart. Believe that He can keep you and live according to His ways."

I thought about what Matthew said, and I found it to be true. Every battle we studied in the Scriptures was in the end about a question of obedience and surrender.

In Joshua , at Ai they lost because of Achan's disobedience. After the fall of Jericho, God told the people to burn everything but save the silver and gold and vessels of iron. But Achan couldn't keep his hands to himself and caused the people to suffer a great loss.

The book of Judges seemed mostly to be a cycle of wins and losses for the nation of Israel. There were battles that involved Israel forsaking their God, and then Jehovah purposely handed the nation over to be defeated by an enemy. Then, when Israel returned to God, He would perform miracles and raise leaders to rescue them.

"But what now, Matthew? What do I do now?"

"Believe, my lord; believe that our God is a rewarder of anyone who seeks Him."

Just when I was about to leave, a young servant burst into the room.

"My lord." He was out of breath.

"What is it, Gaius?"

"Sir, it's the healer, the Messiah, the one named Jesus. He's here in Capernaum."

"He's in our city?"

"Yes sir."

"But … how? Where did he come from?"

"Well, sir, He was in the mountains for a good while teaching many of the people. Most were amazed that He spoke with such authority. It was as if He wrote the Scriptures and not just studied them."

I heard the excitement in Gaius's voice as he caught his breath quickly to continue.

"And then I heard He just cured a man from leprosy by just speaking the word.[10] The report I got was Jesus said, 'I will help you; you are clean,' and the man was made whole. I'm telling you, sir, it's as if He has command over these things."

I looked at Matthew, and my heart lost its strength. I felt helpless and alone. But if the prophet, the master, was here, then there was a chance my servant could live. Matthew was more than a servant to me; he was a guide, an anchor, a spiritual rock.

And that was something I did not want to lose without a fight. But this fight wasn't a battle of swords and shields; this was a battle of faith and belief.

Matthew's body shook vigorously for a minute, and then he opened his eyes and looked up at me.

"What do you believe?" he said. Then he repeated the question again but louder. "What, do you believe?" Then he sank back into a dizzy spell.

"*Oh, dear Lord,*" I prayed, "*I believe You are the one true God, and this same Jesus is the Messiah of the world. Please, Lord, go before me and win this battle. Let my servant live again.*" "Gaius."

---

10 Matthew 8:2–3

"Yes, my lord."

"Take me to the King."

"The King, my lord?"

"Yes, Gaius. Every time the God of Israel goes to battle on behalf of His people, He chooses a King. I believe he has done so again in the one they call Jesus. Take me to the King."

I took two soldiers, and we followed Gaius through the streets. We knew that where the crowds were we would find Jesus. Gaius led and started pushing through the crowd. If I could help it, I didn't want my guards to take active part in dispersing the crowd.

Gaius found Him and told Jesus of the things I had done for the people and explained our reason for coming. Then He beckoned to me, and I took the chance to speak to Him.

"My Lord, I mean You no harm, but I am all out of options and I need Your help. I believe You are a King sent from God. My servant is a good man and loyal to me and all in my house, but he has been struck by a strong illness. I implore, I beg You, my Lord, please heal my servant. Not because he's my servant, but he has become …" I struggled to find the words to describe our relationship. "He has become a mentor, a friend, a guide to me. Please, Lord, he needs You … I … need You."

"That's fine. I will come with you now," said Jesus.

"No, Lord. I know that I'm not worthy for You to enter into my house. I know who I am and I know who You are, but speak the word, just say the word and I know my servant will be healed. I am a man and a soldier. As you can see, I have my guards, and I tell one to go and he goes. I tell another to come and he comes. My power is in no comparison to Yours."

Jesus spoke to the crowd and told them that He had not seen such faith displayed by anyone in Israel. I was so astonished that when He kept on speaking I didn't hear or understand much of what He said. But when He finished, He told me to go back home, as my request was fulfilled.

When we got back home, everyone was in a festive mood. There was music and dancing everywhere.

"Master."

"Matthew, you're up."

"And well, sir. I heard you went to see the Messiah. What happened?"

"Well, I spoke to Him and asked Him to speak the word to heal you, and He said according to my belief you would be."

"About what time was that, sir?"

"I'd say about a half hour ago."

"Well isn't that something," he said. "That's about the same time I started feeling better."

I smiled and let him get back to his friends. Looking down from the balcony at the celebrations going on in the courtyard, all I could say was, "Thank You, Father, for saving him."

Then I heard I quiet whisper as if in reply,

Table Talk

Meanwhile a Jew named Apollos, a native of Alexandria, came to Ephesus. He was a learned man, with a thorough knowledge of the Scriptures. He had been instructed in the way of the Lord, and he spoke with great fervor and taught about Jesus accurately, though he knew only the baptism of John. (Acts 18:24–26)

Have you ever met someone who treated you nicely and then you began to question, *"Okay, what's the catch? What do they want? When are they going to show their real colors?"*

Those are the thoughts that came to mind this morning after I had finished speaking at the synagogue. I had met so many people on my travels, and if truth be told, many have not been so forthcoming. People seem to have their own agenda when they say, "Can I help you, young man?"

I began to get weary of it. However, I did not allow that to deter me from my mission—namely to bring the message of the Messiah, the soon-coming King, just as John the Baptist foretold.

This morning the people were receptive. I received positive comments on my speech, but there lacked something. In my own convictions I knew I was preaching the truth, but when would the Messiah come? How soon? I'd been studying the laws and prophets all my life, but I still felt a void inside.

"Hello, young man, are you all right? You look a bit troubled."

"Oh, I'm sorry, sir. I guess at times I get lost in my thoughts."

"We enjoyed your sermon today. Allow me to introduce myself. I am Aquila, and this is my wife, Priscilla."

"It a pleasure to meet you both. I'm Apollos. I'm originally from Alexandria, but I have been traveling and spreading the good news."

"And what good news is that, my boy?" Aquila asked curiously.

"Well, the good news that the coming of the Messiah is at hand, as John the Baptist preached. The prophet Isaiah said it this way, 'He was despised and rejected by mankind, a man of suffering, and familiar with pain. Like one from whom people hide their faces he was despised, and we held him in low esteem.'"[11]

As I started to recite the passage, I cried a little and then continued. "Can you imagine what the Messiah must go through to redeem humankind?" Aquila and Priscilla stood there and smiled at me; I went on with the quotation.

"Surely he took up our pain and bore our suffering, yet we considered him punished by God, stricken by him, and afflicted."[12]

Then my voice rose as I gained hope of the victory His suffering would bring. "But he was pierced for our transgressions, he was crushed for our iniquities; the punishment that brought us peace was on him, and by his wounds … and by his wounds … and by his wounds … we are healed."[13]

They gave me a moment as they saw I was getting emotional and passionate about the Word of God. Then Priscilla spoke.

"Apollos."

"Yes, Priscilla."

"Where are you staying at Ephesus?"

"I'm not sure. I just arrived and headed straight for the synagogue."

"Then today you stay with us," announced Aquila.

"We insist," said Priscilla with a smile.

It was late afternoon, and after I had a rest, dinner was served.

"Let's hold hands and bless the meal."

I smiled. It was good to be around believing people in a non-temple setting. I felt peaceful. I didn't feel as if I had to be on my guard. It was good.

"Heavenly Father," Aquila started, "thank You for this meal and the opportunity to share it with this servant of Yours. We thank You for making our pathways cross today, and may the fellowship we share be rich and rewarding as much as the meal we are about to partake."

Then he said something I've never heard before. "In Jesus' name, amen."

"Amen," repeated Priscilla.

---

11 Isaiah 53:3
12 Isaiah 53:4
13 Isaiah 53:5

I looked at them respectfully but with a questioning look on my face.

"Um … Aquila … who is Jesus?"

"Remember today when you quoted from the prophet Isaiah."

"Yes, this morning at the synagogue."

"Well, Jesus was the one Isaiah and John spoke of."

Priscilla joined the conversation. "John said, 'I baptize you with water for repentance. But after me comes one who is more powerful than I, whose sandals I am not worthy to carry. He will baptize you with the Holy Spirit and fire. His winnowing fork is in his hand, and he will clear his threshing floor, gathering his wheat into the barn and burning up the chaff with unquenchable fire.'"[14]

"Do you remember these words, Apollos?" asked Priscilla.

"Yes, I do."

"Do you know what happened next?"

"No, I'm not aware of the actual event—only that John preached those words from the banks of the river Jordan."

Priscilla continued. "Witnesses have given us the following account: 'Then Jesus came from Galilee to the Jordan to be baptized by John. But John tried to deter him, saying, "I need to be baptized by you, and do you come to me?" Then Jesus replied, "Let it be so now; it is proper for us to do this to fulfill all righteousness." Then John consented. As soon as Jesus was baptized, he went up out of the water. At that moment heaven was opened, and he saw the Spirit of God descending like a dove and alighting on him. And a voice from heaven said, "This is my Son, whom I love; with him I am well pleased."'"[15]

"Do you understand, Apollos?" Aquila asked. "Jesus. This same Jesus was actually the Messiah. The Son of the living God; He came to fulfill what our fathers of old had faithfully prophesied."

"It was this same Jesus who died on Calvary's hill for our sins—to open the life gate for all to come in," Priscilla joined in.

"I'm beginning to get it now," I said. "What you say ties together with not only what John preached but what he witnessed too."

Then the continued words of Isaiah the prophet came back to me like a mighty flood. "*We all, like sheep, have gone astray, each of us has turned to our own way; and the* L*ORD* *has laid on*

14 Matthew 3:11–12
15 Matthew 3:13–17

him the iniquity of us all. He was oppressed and afflicted, yet he did not open his mouth; He was led like a lamb to the slaughter, and as a sheep before its shearers is silent, so he did not open his mouth. By oppression and judgment he was taken away. Yet who of his generation protested? For he was cut off from the land of the living; for the transgression of my people he was punished. He was assigned a grave with the wicked and with the rich in his death, though he had done no violence, nor was any deceit in his mouth. Yet it was the LORD*'s will to crush him and cause him to suffer, and though the* LORD *makes his life an offering for sin, he will see his offspring and prolong his days, and the will of the* LORD *will prosper in his hand."* (Isaiah 53:6–10)

"Oh my—I have been preaching the baptism of John alone for so long," I exclaimed.

"But that is what you knew," said Priscilla in a sympathizing voice.

"My boy." Aquila's voice was very comforting. "There is nothing for you to feel bad or wrong about. The Lord knows your heart, and it is not by chance that we met today. It was His will for us to share these things with you."

"Thank you for your understanding," I said, feeling relieved and revived.

"Apollos," Priscilla said, taking over, "our heavenly Father understands that there are times we can be sincere about our labors for Him but sincerely wrong. The most important thing is that we learn along this pathway of life."

That evening I returned to the synagogue and preached to the people the more perfect way of salvation through faith in Jesus Christ, the Son of the living God.

Some questioned me as it was just this morning they heard me proclaim the good news of John the Baptist and wondered how I could change so quickly. What I understood from Priscilla and Aquila was that it wasn't a change but rather a development, according to Aquila, "a more perfect way."

After the service I met with my new father and mother in the faith.

"That was wonderful," Priscilla said, smiling. She looked proud of me, and it felt good to be accepted like this.

"Yes, yes, the boy did well," said Aquila, smiling.

"Will you stay a while before you head on?" asked Priscilla.

"Yes, I would like that," I replied, smiling.

"You know something, Apollos," Priscilla started, a bit more settled. "Aquila and I don't have children."

"Priscilla," said Aquila quietly, looking at her from the corner of his eyes.

"Well, I just wanted to say … if we ever had a son … I wish he was just like you." She smiled, and a tear came to her eye.

"Thank you; that's the nicest thing anyone has ever said to me. I haven't seen my parents in such a long time, but I believe they would be relieved and honored to know I was in the company of such good people as you both."

That night as I lay in bed, I reflected over the day and the new revelations I learned of Christ's death and resurrection at Calvary.

"Lord, thank You for leading me to these dear people. I hope more persons in Your church will show the kind of love, care, and patience they have shown me today."

And in the quietness of the night, in the breeze passing by, I heard the words softly spoken:

Torn Between Two Mothers

The woman whose son was alive was deeply moved out of love for her son and said to the king, "Please, my lord, give her the living baby! Don't kill him!" (1 Kings 3:26)

"Ughhhhhhhhhhhhhhhhhhhhhhhhhhh."

"Oh, that doesn't sound too good."

"Do you think we should check on him?"

"Nah, let's give him a few more minutes. Remember he is kind of young—and there are some important people here for him to meet."

No matter how often I went to court, I still felt a bit nervous. My stomach was doing cartwheels, and the guards outside were not enjoying it either.

"Your Majesty."

"Yes."

"Is there anything we can get for you, Your Majesty?"

"No, thank you. I'll just be a minute more." I washed my face and dried my hands.

"Okay, Lord. I asked You for wisdom and understanding, and I believe You have honored my request. Please, help me to honor You and calm down. I could have wisdom and still act in a way that people won't take me seriously. Lord, I need Your Spirit and presence with me."

After that I felt a lot better and joined the two guards outside my door.

"Your Majesty, if you don't mind me saying, we know the Lord is with you, so we are sure you will be fine."

"Yes, Your Majesty, just remember to breathe and you will be okay; and if there is anything you need, we've got your back."

"Yes, Your Majesty, we need to show strength together, so if there is a command you want carried out, even if we don't understand it, we will carry it out."

Isaac and Joel were good soldiers and good men. I knew I had their support, and as a new king, it was good to know I had people around me I could trust.

They followed me as I left my chambers. We walked through the palace and entered the court hall. When we entered the hall, I could see my advisors and members of state sitting near the head throne. As I entered the court, the attendant called out, "All rise, the honorable King Solomon now presiding."

The people stood up, and then I took my seat. Everyone sat down in unison. I acknowledged my advisors and state members with a simple nod of the head.

"Now, on to business," I said.

"Your Majesty," the attendant started "the next case is Mother A versus Mother B."

"Mother A and Mother B?" I questioned. "These women, do they not have names?"

"Yes, Your Honor, but based on the nature of the case and some sensitive issues concerning each woman's affairs, the women requested, if it's acceptable to the court, that their full identities be withheld."

"Okay, I see," I said, sounding a bit unsure of where this was leading. I looked over to Isaac and Joel, but they just gave a slight smile and nod.

"Attendant."

"Yes, Your Majesty."

"Can I hear the details of the case?"

"Yes, your Majesty. Apparently between the hours of seven and eight o'clock yesterday evening, Mother A and Mother B, who both share a single-bedroom dwelling place, went to bed for the night, each with their newborn babies beside them. The following morning Mother A woke up, and according to her statement, the child beside her was still."

"Still?"

"Yes, Your Majesty. Mother A claims no movement came from the baby's body. Upon further investigation she discovered that the baby was deceased. According to her statement, her examination of the child's features concluded that the deceased child was not hers.

"Mother A claims the deceased is Mother B's child and further claims that Mother B went over to Mother A and exchanged her deceased baby with Mother A's live child while she was asleep. Mother B denies this claim and states that the child in her possession is actually hers."

"Yes, I see. Are there any witnesses?"

"No, Your Honor."

"Is the midwife who nursed the children available to make a statement?"

"Your Honor, we have made contact with the midwife, but she cannot recall the ladies' faces, let alone their children as she sees dozens of children and cannot in good conscience identify which mother the child belongs to."

"Well this is something," I said under my breath. "Can I safely assume that both women are in court today?"

"Yes they are, Your Honor."

"Then I will hear statements from both. Mother A, please step forward and give us your version of the events."

Mother A stepped forward and stood in front of me.

"Attendant," I called.

The court attendant came forward with a copy of the Scriptures and asked Mother A to place her hand on it.

"Do you solemnly swear to tell the whole truth, so help you God?" he asked her.

"I do," she replied.

"Please state your name for the court."

"My name is Mother A, and my child was—"

"Stop, madam. We only need your name at this point."

"I'm sorry, sir. My name is Mother A."

"Now, please tell the court your account of the events."

"Well sir, and Your Majesty," she said, bowing to me, "yesterday evening I was in my room with my child, and I had just given him suck. Mother B entered the bedroom with her child. We both shared a room for the convenience. We're not friends or anything. Anyway, that night we both went to sleep with our children, but in the morning when I woke up, there was no movement from the child. When I checked his breathing, the child was dead, my lord."

"Is it possible you lay too close to the child and smothered him yourself?"

"At first I thought so, my lord, but when I examined the child, I could not find the birthmark I noticed when my child was born. And too, my lord, a mother knows the feeling of her newborn. There is a bond that is felt from within. When I looked over at Mother B, the child she had was alive, but even when she tried to give the child suck, the child would not go to her. He cries and cries, Your Majesty, because he knows the woman holding him is not his mother. She must have killed her baby by accident and switched the children before daylight."

"Lies, lies—you just want my baby for yourself. Your Majesty, the child is mine. It's hers who died in the night, and now she wants my baby."

"Order, order in the court," the attendant intervened. The two women went on at each other, each blaming the other for trying to take the live child as their own.

"Stop," I ordered. "I will have a brief recess and then make a decision on the matter."

"All rise," said the attendant. Then the people stood up. I stood up and beckoned to my advisors, and they followed me into a chamber room.

"What are the implications of this case?" I said to the men as I sat down behind the desk.

My advisors were good men. I had three key persons who had served with my father.

"Well, Your Majesty, this case is rather unusual. But a good ruling would help cement your status as king."

"So," I started, "do we have any precedent for this kind of case?"

"My lord, this is not a common case. We have searched the laws, and there is no controversy that is remotely similar in the circumstances."

"Yes, my lord. For example, 'If brothers are living together and one of them dies without a son, his widow must not marry outside the family. Her husband's brother shall take her and marry her and fulfill the duty of a brother-in-law to her. The first son she bears shall carry on the name of the dead brother so that his name will not be blotted out from Israel.'"[16]

"Yes, my lord, in a case like that, the law clearly says what is expected of each party. In a case like this, the judgment will be a first for the people of Israel."

"Okay then, no pressure," I said, smiling. "Thank you, gentlemen."

They left me in the room.

"Well, Lord, I asked You for wisdom, but how will I know I have it until a time comes to actually use it?" I looked up at the ceiling. "Okay, Lord, I am your servant. Be with me now."

16 Deuteronomy 25:5

I left the chamber room and made my way to the main hall, with Isaac and Joel in front.

As we walked, I could only think of the fear the mother of the live child must be going through, trying to prove her child was hers. My mother told me how my father grieved for a child who was ill shortly after birth. She told me how he cried before God, but the child still died. One thing for sure, when a child dies, it causes so much pain to so many people.

But I wonder, if a mother lost her child, would she really take someone else's child knowing she was putting her through the same suffering she went through? Which one carries less pain—to know your child has departed this earth and you bury him and have closure, or to know your child is alive but you don't know where he is and if the person who has him is even taking care of him? One thing for sure—any true mother who lost her child would not wish that pain on anyone else.

We entered the court hall.

"All rise, the honorable King Solomon residing."

The people stood up. I took my seat, and then the people sat—well, the people who had a seat anyway. I started my deliberations.

"Ladies and gentlemen, I have carefully considered the facts of the case and heard statements from both sides. Unfortunately, there are no other witnesses to the case and so it is Mother A's word verses Mother B's word. There is little physical evidence we can use to assist in this case as the only possible person who could help identify which mother is the mother of the child is the midwife. However, as we have heard, the report of the midwife is that she is unable to identify the child due to the sheer volume of children delivered; she cannot sustain that sort of information in an accurate and reliable way.

"The issue here is for the court to determine which mother is the mother of the live child and which is the mother of the deceased one. Unfortunately again, there is no topic or area of law that we can apply to this case as this sort of situation has never materialized in the history of the people of Israel. Because of this, I cannot use a previous judgment to assist to make a current decision.

"Therefore, if there is no area of law that applies, then there is no rule of the law that can be given as there is no area of law that speaks on this matter; and if there is no rule of law, then the law itself cannot be applied to this situation. Thus in conclusion, I cannot use the law to make a decision."

I looked around the court. It was silent; all eyes were fastened on me as if everyone was hanging on to my every word. I took a deep breath to prepare myself for what was to come next.

I looked over to Joel. "Guard."

"Yes, my lord."

"Take up the child."

"Yes, my lord."

Joel acted without hesitation. He stood in front of the women on the middle steps just above where each one was standing.

"Since there is no physical evidence to prove the mother of the child and the law does not in this case support which mother the child should go to, and being the first case of this kind there is no precedent, I hereby command that the child be cut in two and shared between the two women. Guard, draw your sword."

Joel drew his sword.

"My king, my king, no," shouted out Mother A. "Please, my lord, give him to her. I would rather know that my son was alive and not with me than passed from life to death."

"Yes, my lord, you have spoken right," shouted Mother B. "Cut the child in two and let us share the child together."

"No," cried Mother A. She went on her knees and held her stomach with her left hand, reaching out to me with her right arm outstretched, bowing and crying. Anyone could see the pain and anguish this woman was going through.

"Guard."

"Yes, my lord?"

"Give the child to Mother A. A mother's love is a mother's love. No mother who truly knew her baby was alive would want her child put to death."

Joel put back his sword and stepped down and handed the child to the woman who was still on her knees, crying uncontrollably.

I made my way back to my private chambers. Joel and Isaac were in front. As they came to the door, they opened the doors for me and saluted. I stopped at the door and turned to Joel. "Thank you."

"For what, Your Majesty—doing my job? We told you, Your Majesty, you've got this."

"Yes, Your Majesty," Isaac added. "As we said before, we will do your command without hesitation, especially in front of the people."

I smiled and nodded and went inside.

"Thank You, Lord, for being with me today; it was your wisdom and not mine. Will You be with me, Lord, like You were with my father, David? I miss him, Lord; I could have really done with a father today."

And then I heard the Lord's Spirit speak to me. "I am with you, Solomon. Walk with Me, and turn not to the left or to the right … for after all is said and done,

When My Uncle Died

> In the year that King Uzziah died, I saw the Lord, high and exalted, seated on a throne; and the train of his robe filled the temple. (Isaiah 6:1)

I've heard people say there are only two things that are certain in life—death and taxes. Sitting in the courtyard of the palace, decorated with flowers and fine linen drapes, all I could do was watch the visitors, members of the court, and foreign dignitaries and wonder who was genuine and who was putting on an act. Have you ever had people come up to you and say things you didn't want to hear? You look at their faces and don't even recognize who they are.

I was a young man, a prince of the court. My uncle taught me everything I knew about enjoying life to the full. We had parties and music. He taught me how to drink wine, to ride a horse and hold a sword. It was him I told when I had my first kiss. Life was good. And now all I had were a bunch of strangers coming up to me saying, "Don't worry, son. Keep strong; time heals all wounds." The most popular seemed to be, "He was a good man." Words that made me stop and think.

For most of his life, my uncle was a good man. He did what was right in the sight of the Lord. I know he became king in his teens. From what I heard my uncle's dad, King Amaziah, reigned in Judah fifteen years. He found out there was a plot to kill him, so he ran to a place—Lachish, I think was the name of it—but they were either waiting there or someone followed him. I'm not sure about that part of the story, but he was assassinated.

His body was brought back to Jerusalem for burial, and after that, the people choose my uncle. Being king could be hazardous to your health, but my uncle was good at it.

Actually, it was in the latter part of his life that things started to get strange. He had won so many victories and invented so many machines and things for war that I could see the change in him. He thought he was above everyone and everything.

But a time came when he thought he was more righteous than the priests. He went into the temple where the priests conducted the services for the Lord and wanted to burn incense on the altar. Azariah, who was the head priest, followed in after him, along with eighty other priests who were determined to stop him.

When they confronted my uncle, they reminded him of the history of the Jewish temple—that it was the priests' job as the descendants of Aaron to serve the Lord there. It was their duty to burn incense before the Lord, not his. This was a bad move and one that dishonored God.

You'd have thought my uncle would have humbled himself, asked for forgiveness, and put his tail between his legs and get out of there, but not him. On top of having a censer in his hand ready to burn incense, he became angry and argued and shouted at the priests while they were doing their job—protecting the temple from threats, both foreign and domestic.

While he was having a go at the priests, the leprosy broke out in his forehead. They ushered him out quickly. In fact he himself was anxious to leave, but by that time it was too late.

I remember a conversation my uncle and I had one day after that episode.

"Boy."

"Yes, Uncle."

"When you're on the throne, you have to do everything you can to hold on to your power."

"But Uncle, aren't we supposed to be a holy nation? Aren't we supposed to follow the laws of our fathers?"

"My boy, my dear, dear boy, in time you will realize that the only person you can rely on is you. The prophets, the scribes, the lawmakers—they answer to me, not me to them."

"Do you really believe that, Uncle? Who gave you the victories and military might? Wasn't it our God?"

He didn't answer.

"And now, who gave you the leprosy? Wasn't it the same God who gave you the victories? And why? Because you were too full of yourself, that's why."

He turned his face away from me.

My uncle had grown callous and cold when it came to the holy places. I often wondered if that was a good thing to follow, but then, he was my uncle and my mentor. I just didn't know.

I guess I didn't want to upset him.

Was this the way he wanted to be remembered as king? After all the good he'd done, only to finish his race like this?

No, there must be more to life than this—at least I hoped there was.

Shock

But now I was sitting in the courtroom, just looking into space, thinking of the time I first got the news. I heard it from his personal attendant.

"Isaiah."

"Yes sir, how are you today?" I said, being cordial.

"Isaiah, he's gone."

"Who's gone?" I knew what he was talking about, but I just went into denial.

"The king is gone. He passed away earlier this morning, before daylight."

Tears started to stream down my face. I remember standing there motionless while the words began to sink in. "Where is he? I want to see him."

He led me to the king's bedchamber. A few people were there, standing in and outside the room. I walked up to the lifeless body lying in his bed.

I looked at him and just stared. I knew he was sick, and I knew this day was coming, but somewhere in the back of my mind, I hoped for mercy and that he would be healed.

Control

"Okay, Isaiah, keep it together. Don't freak out now; there are people who are looking to you so be strong. Be strong … be strong." What does that really mean, "be strong"? Be strong to carry out the funeral plans or be strong to be a comfort to other people, especially the younger relatives?

Well, one thing taking part in the preparations did for me was to accept that my uncle had really passed on. I guess for me it was a way of working stuff out so I felt a release as it were of built-up feelings I couldn't explain. I preferred that than someone, with good intentions, mind you, trying to keep me away until the funeral. This way I could deal with it better, by being a part of everything.

Regression

After the funeral, I became very withdrawn. Some family members had to leave, including well-wishers and friends. That's the thing with a funeral—it brings together people you know, but you don't get the chance for all to come together under one roof.

When the service was over and the dinner eaten and the speeches and tributes spoken, people went back to living their normal lives.

My normal would never be the same again. I wondered how the smaller children were taking it. They were playing tag in the courtyard. I guess they never really understood what had just happened. I looked at them and wondered how blissful they must be at that tender age. I also felt angry that they weren't crying and showing remorse. The feelings I had could not be trusted.

But kids are kids. I wondered at their understanding of loss. They didn't cry at the funeral, but when their parents were leaving and started separating friends and cousins, they started to cry because that relationship was about to be broken. All I could do was look on and smile.

Anger

Walking around the palace, I tried to remember things we did together, conversations we had in different places. As I walked I could feel the anger rising inside me. One day I went to his grave.

"Why did you have to die?" I shouted. "Why did you leave me?" I was snapping and biting at everyone. I really didn't mean it, and after a harsh word came out, it was difficult to apologize.

Then one day I saw Azariah, the head priest. "It's your fault … it's your fault the king's dead," I shouted.

"Isaiah, you know better than that."

"It's your fault," I cried again. Then he held me as I cried.

Guilt

"Maybe if I was with him I could have stopped him", I thought to myself. "*He would have listened to me.*"

I kept playing over what happened in the temple and where I was at the time. *"Maybe if I had been there … Maybe if I had known what he had in mind …"*

I had a lot of maybes, but there was only one outcome. My uncle had died. Maybe one may look on his passing as an untimely death.

"If he had just ...

"Maybe if I ... he would be alive.

"Maybe!"

Denial

For some reason or another, I kept looking into the throne room to see if he was there sitting on the throne. I visited our favorite places, hoping to see if it was just a trick to foil his enemies. All kings had enemies; maybe this was a way to outsmart them.

I even went walking on the city walls, where he had designed multiple bows that shot lots of arrows at a time.

He loved his inventions; maybe I'd see him there.

"Yes. Was that his voice? There was a person who looked like him. Was that him?"

No. My uncle, my mentor, my king was gone.

Loneliness

When my heart began to accept that he wasn't coming back, I started to feel as if there was a void, an empty spot in my life that couldn't be replaced. It was funny and strange at the same time. I would be walking in the courtyard where we used to walk and discuss things about life. He seemed to know something about everything—the kingdom, politics, history, family, and wealth—but as I walked, I realized those talks we had would never happen anymore.

My family thought it was time for me to stop grieving and move on, so they invited some family friends and friends of mine over for dinner. The shell of me was there, but my heart and soul were somewhere else. I was surrounded by all these well-wishing people, people I knew had a genuine interest and concern for my health, but in the middle of the crowd, I had never felt so lonely in all my life.

I fell sick. I was standing in the rain one night looking up at the stars. By the time I came in and went to bed, I was roasting with fever.

"Oh Isaiah." my mother started. "I know you miss him. You and your uncle were so close, but do you think this is what he would have wanted?"

I looked up at her, squeezed my eyes tight, and gently shook my head.

"He had a thing for life you know. He would have wanted you to live yours and not try to end it. Why do you think he accomplished so much?"

She was right. My uncle did love life. He was always inventing, always thinking, and always trying something new. It killed him, trying something new. Some new things are not always good things, but that was him. That was my uncle

Adaptation

When I got better, I decided within myself that it was time to start living again. I couldn't forget my uncle, oh no. But I accepted that what was done was done. I took small steps and started to do things one day at a time, like read the laws, study literature, visit a friend.

Then finally, I decided to visit the temple. At first I stood from a distance. Then each day I got nearer and nearer.

I think that with each time I got closer, I realized even more it wasn't God's fault that my uncle died, but it was his own conceit and pride.

Then one day I went in. I was greeted by Azariah.

"How are you, young man?"

"I'm getting there, sir."

"Well it's good to see you up and about again; I heard you were ill recently."

"Thank you, sir. I am feeling a lot better now."

"If there is anything we can do for you, just let us know," he said with a genuine smile.

"Well actually, sir, there is." I felt a bit awkward, but he really seemed to understand. "Is it okay if I sit here at the back for a while?"

"Of course, son; take all the time you need." Then he left.

"Lord, I'm sorry for what my uncle did ... and I'm sorry for blaming You for his ... You know. I'm just tired, Lord, and I want to start living again. I am sorry for how I've acted lately, and I just wanted to know if You would forgive me. I loved my uncle, Lord, but I don't want to end up like him."

Then I saw the most wonderful vision. It was as if heaven itself opened up before my eyes.

"Lord, are you going to show me these wonderful things, things too wonderful for me to even speak?"

"Stay with me, My child, and let me show you a glimpse of glory. For after all is said and done,

You Won't Be Touched

"Now then, please swear to me by the LORD that you will show kindness to my family, because I have shown kindness to you. Give me a sure sign that you will spare the lives of my father and mother, my brothers and sisters, and all who belong to them—and that you will save us from death." (Joshua 2:12–13)

Rahab was my eldest daughter. She was smart and beautiful and had such a lovely spirit. I really wanted her to find someone nice to marry, but instead of thinking about herself and her future, all she could put first was her family. She was a blessing to have, but as her Father, wasn't it my job to take care of her rather than she take care of me?

And so another argument brewed.

"You're killing me with what you're doing. I'm your father; I'm the one who's supposed to provide for you, not you for me."

"Dad, we have to eat. It's not your fault we had a stroke of bad luck. But look at it—Mom can't work, and the children are too young to do anything to earn. It's just until we get back on our feet as a family."

Things have really been tough lately, especially since I had my accident.

There was work in Jericho. The city was well enough with business. The walls were our protection from the outside world, and it seemed nothing could happen without anyone knowing. And yet, in my own home things were getting harder and harder. I fell off a balcony at work recently and broke my leg. Money got tight, and that's when my Rahab came up with her plan for support. She was a determined young woman, I'll give her that.

To see her grow before my eyes and sacrifice herself to put the family first was a burden she wasn't born to bear. But I was growing tired of arguing—and all it seemed to do was make matters worse.

"Dad, I know you're worried, but I'll be all right. I can handle myself, you know," she said, smiling.

"That's what worries me," I said wearily. "You can handle yourself all too well. I don't want to see you do anything that will jeopardize your future of having a family of your own one day."

"If I sense danger, I know how to get out; besides, most of the time, it's the company people want. We just sit and talk, and they tell me things."

"Like what things?" my wife asked. She was in the kitchen making supper.

"Well, I've heard these wonderful stories about the children of Israel and how their God made the waters of the Red Sea part in two so they could walk on dry land. Some say He blew the sea apart with the strength of His breath."

"Yes, I've heard of such stories," I added. "A lot of people are worried that the Israelites will do to us like they did to the Amorite kings of the East.[17] Their God is powerful—maybe more powerful than Jericho's walls."

"Father."

"Yes, my child."

"I do love you—you know that, don't you? I never intended to hurt you or Mother."

I held my head down and tried to hide the tears, but they came anyway.

"I have an idea Mica," Mother volunteered. "Why don't we go and visit your brother? It has been a while, and it will give you both a chance to catch up."

I looked up and smiled. "That's good. We can even go tomorrow. You're right, it has been a while, and one thing with him—he seems to be in the place where all the latest news is shared first, so I'm sure we'll get an update on what's happening in the city."

"Dad."

"Yes, my dear."

"If we were attacked by the Israelite people, do you think their God would spare us?"

I stopped to consider Rahab's question. "Baby, from what I've heard, the God of the Israelites goes before them and fights their battles, but it is also my understanding that He is passionate for people to walk in His ways. You never know, maybe He will—and maybe He won't. But for now, let's have supper."

In the morning we started packing to visit my brother Daniel. Everyone was moving around except Rahab.

---

17 Numbers 21:21–26

"Rahab, I don't see you packing anything. Where are your things?"

"Father, I can't come with you this time to visit Uncle Daniel."

"What? Why are you saying this? They love you over there. You know you're his favorite niece."

"Father, I have to work tonight. I can't afford to lose my … business. I'm sorry, but please give my best to the family, and we'll see each other soon."

I knew by now there was no point in arguing with her. Most times it led to unintended words being said that you couldn't take back, so I accepted it and moved on.

"One day, Rahab, it won't be like this. We will be a family again—a real family."

"Dad, we are a real family—just one with real problems to work out," she said, smiling.

After we said our good-byes, we made our way through the streets. You could feel the tension in the air as talk of a possible invasion seemed to be on everyone's lips.

"Ahhhhhhh …" my brother said softly. "Welcome, brother, welcome."

"It's good to see you too, Daniel."

"Martha, you look as lovely as ever."

"You always were the charmer, Daniel, but it's still nice to hear. You look well. How are the boys?" Martha asked, smiling.

It was a good idea to visit; the break was something we all needed.

"They're fine. It was just the other day we were wondering when we were going to see you all again."

We finished our greeting and carried our things into the house. My brother didn't live in an apartment on the wall like we did. He had a house in the city, just outside the market area. There was a lot of hustle and bustle going on.

"Hello, children, it's good to see you again."

"Hello, Uncle Daniel," they sang in a chorus, smiling.

My brother was the only remaining family we had with his two teenage sons. It's funny how life can be. He always wanted girls but got boys; I wanted boys and got girls before the youngest, my son, was born.

The only sad thing was his wife had passed away a few years back. We encouraged him to move on, but I guess he just wasn't ready. He had a lot of love to give, but for now, he was just content raising his sons.

"Where are the boys now?" I asked.

"You hold on, before we get to them—where is my Rahab? Why isn't she with you?"

I gave Martha an awkward look, pressing my lips together.

"She couldn't be here today, but she does send her love." Martha tried to sound positive, but my brother was more sensitive than that.

"Okay, you girls, why don't you two go and find your cousins? They're out by the stalls."

"Okay, Uncle." They kissed us and left.

"Okay, big brother. What's going on?"

It made no sense trying to hide it any longer. "Well, since my accident things have been harder on us than I let you know. Rahab has been helping, but what she has put herself through, just for us to get by, has come at a great sacrifice."

"I understand, but why didn't you say something to me? If we're the only family we've got, then don't we have to try and stick together?"

We talked all that afternoon but found no real solutions. That night we all stayed up late, playing and laughing, way into the night. It was good to see the children having fun. It reminded me of better days. And then, just before we were settling off for bed, a call came at the door.

"Daniel, Daniel open up. There's something you need to hear."

The man kept banging on the door, and then my brother answered.

"Who's there? Jacob, is that you?"

"Yes, open the door … and hurry before someone sees me."

Jacob was my brother's neighbor. We knew him, but we weren't close in any way.

"Jacob, what's going on? Do you know what time of night it is?"

"Listen to me. Soldiers, the king's soldiers, were at your brother's house earlier."

Martha and I came closer. He had our attention.

"Soldiers," I repeated. "Rahab—is my daughter all right? If anyone has hurt her …"

"Hold on, brother. Let the man speak. Jacob, tell us what's happened."

"Well, from what I've heard on the streets, two spies came through the city earlier this evening and found their way to your brother's house. Someone saw them and told the guards."

"So what happened to Rahab?" asked Martha while holding on to me. I could feel her grip tightening around my arm.

"The guards came to the house, but the spies had already left."

"Enough," I shouted. "Daniel, we need to go."

"No, Mica," said Jacob. "I know you're worried for your daughter, but the city is under curfew. From what I've heard, she is safe. She has not been harmed in any way. But the city is on lockdown. No one is allowed in or out of the gates, and soldiers are patrolling the streets, ordering everyone to remain inside their doors."

"But what of my daughter?" I said, my voice almost breaking.

"As I said, she's not harmed in any way. The guards tried to find the spies, but it seems they slipped away. When they couldn't find them, they put two soldiers to guard your door in case they tried to double back. Trust me, Mica—if you leave now, the only thing that will happen is you'll get yourself arrested."

"Then you leave at first light," my brother said.

We thanked Jacob for the news of Rahab's safety and for warning us about the curfew. After a while everyone went back to bed, but we were all too on edge to sleep.

"Mica."

"Yes, Martha."

"I'm worried for Rahab; do you think she's all right?"

"She's stronger than me—and smarter than you. If anyone knows how to handle this situation, it's her."

As daylight came, we headed back to our home.

"Brother, keep in touch. And let me know what's happened."

"I will, Daniel. I will. Besides, you may see us sooner than you think."

As we headed through the streets, I could feel eyes looking at us.

"Ignore them," Martha said. "The sooner we get home, the better."

"Rahab."

"Mom, Dad, I have so much to tell you."

"Are you all right?" Martha asked as we all ran and hugged her tight. "We heard the news last night."

"Did they hurt you?" asked the children.

"No, I'm fine."

She told us how the spies had come to the house and how she hid them in the loft when the guards came looking for them; then made a way for them to escape by climbing down the city wall.

"There's something else," she continued. "I made a pact with the spies. I asked them that since I helped them escape, in return when their people attacked the city, they would spare my family and our relatives."

"I told you she's smart," I said to Martha.

"But how will they know where we are?" asked Martha.

"Oh, they gave me this red rope and told me to hang it outside our window facing the fields. That's the sign to protect our home."

"Daniel and the boys," I said nervously.

"Dad, we need to get word to Uncle and let them come and stay with us. They'll only be safe under our roof."

After we unpacked, we started preparations to receive my brother and the boys.

"Dad, we're going to be okay, aren't we?"

"Well, the men gave their word that we wouldn't be harmed, and one thing I do believe, if they gave their word by their God then we will be saved. And besides, if He protects us now, then I'm sure He will provide for us after the battle. We're looking at a new life ahead."

I smiled, feeling more confident about the future. It's strange that even though I knew danger was coming, along with it came the hope of a new beginning.

"Yes, Dad," Rahab said with a smile. "But that's not what I'm talking about. Are we—you and me—are we going to be okay?"

At that moment I saw the little girl I knew and loved. Once again tears came down my face, but these weren't tears of pain; these were tears of joy. I went over to her, and we hugged each other close.

"Of course we are okay, baby girl. After all …

Part 4
An Easter Story

It is winding down to the last hours before the cross. The angels are anxious about the unjust punishment Christ will suffer.

Even though the book is already written, they are still concerned for the Son of God, Jesus.

Gabriel has been assigned to follow Jesus as He lives His final hours. Starting at the Last Supper, his job is to relay a commentary of the proceedings to the angels led by the archangel Michael.

As the sequence of events unfold, Gabriel and the angels are amazed at the level of betrayal Jesus is exposed to, even from people He considered His closest friends.

At one point all seems lost, only to realize a wonderful lesson, that when all is said and done, the Father is still on the throne and though weeping may endure through the night, joy does come in the morning.

The Assignment

"How will this be," Mary asked the angel, "since I am a virgin?" The angel answered, "The Holy Spirit will come on you, and the power of the Most High will overshadow you, so the holy one to be born will be called the Son of God." (Luke 1:34–35)

It's been almost thirty-three years since I last stepped foot on planet earth. The last time was a sad and joyous occasion. We all knew Jesus was to leave the presence of the Father and take off His divinity and glory so the Holy Spirit could carry Him to earth to be born of Mary.

Mary—I remember how young she looked when we first met. I wonder how she looks now. Jesus was the only person worthy enough to be the ultimate sacrifice to redeem the souls of men. No animal or person was perfect enough.

"Gabriel."

"Oh, hello, Michael. I must have wandered off in thought."

"That's okay. The Father is asking for you."

"Is something wrong?"

"I'm not sure. Only God knows." Michael smiled.

We walked together, and then we came to the throne room. The doors opened, and we walked in toward the throne. Michael and I stopped a short way before and bowed our heads.

"Come forward, Gabriel."

I left Michael's side and took a few steps nearer to the throne.

"Yes, my Lord."

"Gabriel, I have an assignment for you. The book has been written from beginning to end; however, the angels do not know the full story."

"Yes, my Lord. As I recall, the book was written between Yourself, the Son, and the Holy Spirit."

"The angels serving here would like to know if they could receive a commentary of the last events of Jesus's time on earth. How about you going down and keeping them informed?"

"I would be honored, my Lord."

"There is a stipulation."

"Yes, my Lord."

"You cannot reveal yourself to a mortal soul. Without My consent, no earthly being must know you are there, and under no circumstance are you to interfere with proceedings. Do you understand, Gabriel?"

"Yes, my Lord, I understand. When do I leave?"

"Well, they are about to have their last supper together, so now would be a good time to begin and cover the events leading up to … leading up to …"

As the Father spoke I could see the hurt in His eyes as He knew what was to come.

"Yes, my Lord. I will leave now."

The Last Supper

Thursday Night between 6:00 p.m. and 9:00 p.m.

> When the hour came, Jesus and his apostles reclined at the table. And he said to them, "I have eagerly desired to eat this Passover with you before I suffer. For I tell you, I will not eat it again until it finds fulfillment in the kingdom of God." (Luke 22:14–16)

When I arrived at the upper room, the table was already set and Jesus was eating with His disciples. At first they observed the Passover meal in commemoration of the freedom from slavery the Father performed for Moses and the children of Israel.

That was a very desperate time. The plagues the Father unleashed on Pharaoh and the Egyptians did not convince them to let Israel go. Then finally, the Lord told Moses that He would pass through every house of the Egyptians and would take the life of every firstborn of people and animals in judgment.[18]

As for the nation of Israel, each family was to take a lamb from its flock, prepare it for a meal, and take the blood and paint the top and sides of the doorposts. The Lord told them that wherever He saw the blood, He would pass over that house, and all would be safe.

After the Passover meal, Jesus took wine and bread and gave thanks. This was a new thing.

"Gabriel, what's happening?"

"Well, Michael, it seems Jesus is implementing a new supper service. He's taken a cup of wine and told the disciples to drink all of it. Now Jesus has given the disciples bread and told them to divide it among themselves."

"What does that mean?"

---

18 Exodus 12:12–13

"He's saying the cup is a symbol of His blood and the bread is a symbol of His broken body. There's more—He will not eat this again with them until the kingdom of God comes."

"Gabriel, do you think they understand what is about to happen?"

"I don't think so, Michael. Jesus is telling them that He is about to be betrayed by someone in the group, but all they are thinking of is who among them will be the greatest."

"I see, and now?"

"Jesus is talking to Simon Peter. Peter is declaring that he is willing to go with Jesus to prison and even death if needs be. But Jesus says he will betray Him three times before the night is over. Michael, it doesn't look good. Everything Jesus is trying to teach them seems to be like water running off a duck's back."

"That's sad. How will Jesus cope if He doesn't have any support? What is He saying to them now?"

"Jesus is reminding them that when He sent them out with no provisions, they lacked nothing, but now if they have a purse, take it, including a bag. He's saying if they don't have a sword, they should sell their coat and buy one. I think He's showing them the importance of having the Scriptures with them. Jesus knows His time is near."

"So what are the disciples saying in reply, Gabriel?"

"It looks like they believe Jesus was talking about actual fighting swords, like what the Romans use and not the Scriptures. He is tired, trying to teach them. He has had enough for now."

Gethsemane
Thursday Night between 9:00 p.m. and Midnight

> Then Jesus went with his disciples to a place called Gethsemane, and he said to them, "Sit here while I go over there and pray." (Matthew 26:36)

"Okay, Michael, I'm on location in Gethsemane. Jesus is here with the disciples, but hold on a minute—I count eleven men; someone is missing. It's Judas; he's the one who's going to betray Jesus. I didn't see that coming."

"So, Gabriel, eleven disciples remain. What is Jesus doing there?"

"Well, He has told eight of the disciples to stay nearby, and He's taking Peter, James, and John further into the garden."

"He always did have an inner circle He wanted to depend on when things got difficult, Gabriel."

"Yes, like the time when He took them apart and led them up a high mountain, met with Elijah and Moses, and transfigured Himself before them."[19]

"Yes, Gabriel, I remember."

"Jesus just told the three men to stay with Him. Let's see if I can hear what He's saying."

"My soul is overwhelmed with sorrow to the point of death. Stay here and keep watch with me."

"Michael, Jesus is really distraught. I'm not sure if He can handle the pain of the cross in His human body. I want to help Him, but the Father said I can't interfere. Wait a minute; I believe He's praying to the Father now."

"My Father, if it is possible, may this cup be taken from me. Yet not as I will, but as you will."

---

19 Mark 9:2

Three times Jesus prayed this prayer with no support from His disciples. It was just one of those times you wish someone had your back. But He was so lonely and broken, and each time He went back to check on the disciples, they were sleeping. I could not intervene, but I could offer a word of encouragement.[20]

"Gabriel, there's still no answer from the throne."

"I know, Michael; He needs to find the strength to carry out the Father's will."

---

20 Luke 22:43

The Arrest
Friday between Midnight and 3:00 a.m.

Then the detachment of soldiers with its commander and the Jewish officials arrested Jesus. They bound him and brought him first to Annas, who was the father-in-law of Caiaphas, the high priest that year. (John 18:12–13)

"Wait, what's this? A crowd of people are coming to the garden led by. … I think it's Judas. Yes, it's him."

"Gabriel, who is it? Who's there with Judas?"

"It looks like a unit of soldiers and people from the chief priests, including scribes and elders. They are armed with weapons and carrying torches and lanterns. It looks like they are out to arrest Jesus."

"That's crazy. What has Jesus done to deserve this?"

"I know, Michael; it looks more like a witch hunt than a gathering for the Son of God. Hold on, Jesus is speaking."

"Who do you want?"

"Jesus of Nazareth."

"I am He."

"Gabriel?"

"Jesus just said, 'I am He,' and the people who came for Him fell to the ground, including Judas. Jesus is asking them again."

"I ask you again, who do you want?"

"Jesus of Nazareth."

"I told you that I am He. If you are looking for Me, then let these men go."

"Gabriel what's happening? What are they doing to Jesus?"

"They're going toward Him to arrest Him. Wait … Peter is taking up a sword; I think he is trying to defend Jesus."

"What is he thinking? We're ready to come to his aid."

"Oh no!"

"What?"

"Peter just cut off a man's ear. Jesus is talking to him."

"Put your sword away! Shall I not drink the cup the Father has given me?"

"Michael, Jesus just healed the man's ear and is willingly giving Himself over to the crowd."

"Then Gabriel, it's a part of the Master's plan."

"It seems so, Michael. It seems so."

The House of Caiaphas
Early Friday Morning between 3:00 a.m. and 6:00 a.m.

Then seizing him, they led him away and took him into the house of the High Priest. Peter followed at a distance. (Luke 22:4)

"Gabriel, where are they taking Jesus?"

"They're taking Him to the house of Caiaphas, the high priest. It seems they want to have some kind of trial about His claim to be the Son of the living God."

"But He is."

"Yes, we know that, Michael, but these men, something is terribly wrong. They claim to be the spiritual leaders of the temple and hear from our Father for the direction of the people. But to them, the temple has become a place of prominence and power; they wouldn't know the voice of God even if He did speak to them."

"So, where are the disciples? Are any of them with Him?"

"The only one in my sight is Peter, and he's following from a distance. Hold on. Well now, would you believe this?"

"What is it Gabriel? What's happening?"

"Could you ever imagine, Peter was just sitting by a fire in the middle of the courtyard and a young servant girl came and asked him if he was one of Jesus's followers?"

"So, what did Peter say?"

"He said he didn't know the man. Hold on, it's happening again. This time a man is asking."

"You also are one of them, yes. You are a follower of Jesus?"

"Man, I am not!"

"Michael, I think Peter is losing it."

"Gabriel, in fairness, it seems like all the disciples have lost it."

About an hour later another person confronted Peter.

"Certainly this fellow was with him, for he is a Galilean."

"Man, I don't know what you're talking about!"

"Michael."

"Yes, Gabriel."

"Jesus did tell Peter this would happen. It's about six in the morning, and a rooster just crowed. I think Peter now remembers the words himself."

"Why, what has he done?"

"Well, Jesus just turned and looked straight at him, and Peter went outside and started to cry."

Before Pilate

Very early in the morning, the chief priests, with the elders, the teachers of the law and the whole Sanhedrin, made their plans. So they bound Jesus, led him away and handed him over to Pilate. (Mark 15:1)

"More people are gathering. It looks like Caiaphas's house was just a meeting place for them to devise their plan to get rid of Jesus, and now they're putting it into action."

"Gabriel, what are they doing now?"

"They're moving Jesus from Caiaphas's house and taking him to Pontius Pilate for questioning."

"Pilate?"

"Remember, Michael, Pilate is the fifth prefect for the Roman-governed province of Judaea. No trial or sentence can be carried out without his approval."

"I see."

"Pilate is questioning Jesus now."

"Are You the king of the Jews?"

"You have said so."

"Aren't You going to answer? Don't You see how many things they are accusing You of?"

"Gabriel, what is Jesus saying?"

"Michael, He's not saying a word. He is as quiet as a lamb. Now Pilate is speaking to the chief priests."

"Do you want me to release to you the king of the Jews?"

"Michael, the chief priests are really tricky."

"What do you mean?"

"They are not answering Pilate directly but stirring up the crowd to pressure Pilate to release Barabbas instead. Can you hear their chants?"

"No, give us Barabbas, give us Barabbas."

"Now Pilate is addressing the crowd instead of the priests."

"What shall I do, then, with the one you call the 'king of the Jews'?"

"Crucify Him!"

"Why? What crime has He committed?"

"Crucify Him!"

Sent to Herod

On hearing this, Pilate asked if the man was a Galilean. When he learned that Jesus was under Herod's jurisdiction, he sent him to Herod, who was also in Jerusalem at that time. (Luke 23:6–7)

"Michael, I have a bad feeling about this."

"Gabriel, what's Pilate planning to do?"

"It looks like he just wants to wash his hands from everything. He's about to speak to the guards."

"Captain."

"Yes, my lord."

"Where is this man from?"

"I believe it is Galilee, my lord."

"Galilee—isn't that under Herod's jurisdiction?"

"Yes, my lord, it is."

"Well then, send Him to Herod, and let him deal with Him."

"Yes, my lord, as you wish. Guards, escort the prisoner out."

Returned to Pilate

Then Herod and his soldiers ridiculed and mocked him. Dressing him in an elegant robe, they sent him back to Pilate. (Luke 23:11)

"Gabriel, where are you now?"

"Well, Pilate is trying to get out of judging Jesus because he knows He is an innocent man. Even though he and Herod don't get on, Pilate has sent Jesus to Herod for him to deal with. Listen."

"So this is the man they call Jesus. They say You are the king of the Jews. What say You?"

"Gabriel?"

"Michael, again Jesus is not saying a thing. Now Herod is asking Jesus a barrage of questions. The chief priests and teachers are strongly accusing Him of stirring up trouble in the province, and now even the soldiers have joined in. Herod and the soldiers are mocking Jesus, and they've put a robe on Him as if He is a pretend king. It's humiliating."

"Send Him back to Pilate; I've had enough fun for one day."

Sentenced

But with loud shouts they insistently demanded that he be crucified, and their shouts prevailed. So Pilate decided to grant their demand. (Luke 23:23–24)

"Gabriel, you're back at Pilate's hall?"

"Michael, it just does not seem to stop. Three times … three times, Pilate pleaded with the people to release Jesus as both he and Herod found no reason for Him to be put to death. The people have just rejected Jesus outright and are adamant He be crucified. I think Pilate fears that if he doesn't do something to appease the crowd, there is going to be a riot, and that will not look good to Rome on his watch. It looks like he has made a decision."

"Captain."

"Yes, my lord."

"Have Barabbas released from his cell."

"Yes, my lord, and what of the king of the Jews? My lord? The Jew?"

"Michael, Pilate is looking at Jesus now and wondering what to do."

"Flog Him, and hand Him over to be crucified. That should be enough for the people."

"Yes, my lord."

The Crucifixion
Friday 6:00 a.m. to 9:00 a.m.

It was nine in the morning when they crucified him. The written notice of the charge against him read: THE KING OF THE JEWS. (Mark 15:25–26)

"So, Gabriel, in an unusual twist of events, the Son is going to die on a cross."

"Oh, Michael, I know it has to be done, but I never thought it would be like this."

"How is Jesus now?"

"I thought it was bad enough He had been publically humiliated, but the soldiers have beaten Him near to death. And now they've given Him His own cross to carry, and He's stumbling with it."

"Can't they at least carry it for Him?"

"No; wait, look. The soldiers just took hold of a passerby; he says his name is Simon of Cyrene. They're forcing him to help Jesus carry the cross to Golgotha. Now they're offering Jesus wine mixed with myrrh to dull the pain, but He's refusing it. He wants to be conscious throughout the whole ordeal."

"Gabriel, Jesus is stronger than any of us could have imagined."

"Yes, Michael, you are right, but I fear the worst is still to come. There are two other men who are going to be crucified with Jesus. They're being led out with Him."

"Is He saying anything, Gabriel?"

"Well, He did give a prophetic word of warning on the way up the hill to women who were weeping for Him. He told them that an even greater time of judgment would come, and at that time, there would be nowhere to run."

"Gabriel, have they arrived?"

"Yes, they just put up Jesus with His arms stretched out on the cross, and the two criminals are hanging one on each side of Him. Hold on, He's about to say something."

"Father, forgive them, for they do not know what they are doing."

"Well Michael, it's about nine in the morning, and the final nail has been hammered in and the cross is set firmly in the ground."

"What's happening around Him?"

"The soldiers have taken His robe, but on examination of it they realized that it has no seam. It's one piece of woven cloth, so rather than tear it and spoil it, they're gambling to see who can win it."

"Gambling at the foot of the cross? Are you telling me that these men have no form of remorse?"

"Michael, none whatsoever."

The Crucifixion
Friday 9:00 a.m. to Noon

"Well, Michael, would you believe this."

"Gabriel, what's happening now?"

"The chief priests, the same ones who orchestrated this whole conspiracy—it's not enough that they had Jesus put to death. Now they're coming round and throwing insults at Him and taunting Him to prove He is the Son of God by coming down from the cross. It's sad. Michael, I'm glad you're not here. You wouldn't believe how people are jumping on the bandwagon to humiliate Jesus."

"Gabriel, who else is at the cross making fun of Him?"

"There are some soldiers who are saying, 'If You are the king of the Jews, save Yourself,' and they still want Him to drink the wine and vinegar."

"Gabriel, what about the other men crucified on each side of Jesus? Are they as nonchalant as the priests and the soldiers?"

"Michael, it's an amazing thing. Both of these men are guilty of the crimes laid against them, but they seem to have two totally different attitudes toward Jesus. Hear the one on the left for yourself."

"Aren't You supposed to be the Messiah? Then why are You still here? Save Yourself, and while You're at it, You can save us too."

"He's bitter."

"I told you, brother. There's hardly any compassion around the Son at all."

"Well, Gabriel, what about the other man? What's his story?"

"Listen to this."

"Hey, show some respect. We deserve to be here, but this man has done nothing wrong to have this punishment. Lord, please remember me when You enter into Your kingdom."

"I tell you, today you will be with Me in paradise."

"Gabriel, is there anyone there in Jesus's corner? Is there anyone there supporting Him?"

"Well, there's Mary, Jesus's mother, Mary Magdalene, who anointed Him with the alabaster box of oil, and the mother of James and John, Zebedee's sons."

"What about the seventy[21] He gave powers to and sent out to do the work of the Father and preach the kingdom of God is at hand? Are any of the seventy present?"

"Michael, I'm sorry, but they have long left Jesus's side."

"Okay then, what of the twelve, or should I say eleven? Surely they must be near Him now?"

"Well, as for Judas, when he realized he betrayed innocent blood, he went out and hung himself. The rest of disciples have scattered. From the twelve, He took three, and from the three, there is only one standing at the cross—John."

"Then, Gabriel, say the word, and I will have twelve legions[22] of angels there to protect the Son of God."

"Michael, I understand how you feel, but this is not our fight. Jesus must bear this alone. Now he's looking down at the small group of people here to mourn Him. He's gathering His strength to speak. He's looking at His mother, Mary."

"Woman, here is your son."

"And now he's speaking to John."

"Here is your mother."

---

21 Luke 10:1
22 Matthew 26:53

The Crucifixion
Friday Noon to 3:00 p.m.

"Michael."

"Yes, Gabriel."

"What's happening? It's just midday, but the sky is turning as dark as night."

"We'll just have to wait and see."

"Michael, three hours have passed, and it's still dark. Wait a minute—Jesus is about to say something. I think we're coming close to the end."

"Gabriel."

"Hold on, Michael. Jesus is about to say something."

"*Eli, Eli, lema sabachthani*?"

"Michael, He said, 'My God, My God, why have You forsaken Me?' Where is the Father?"

"The Father is here, but He cannot look on His Son now. Jesus is taking upon Himself the sins of the whole world. I never realized the burden would be so great."

"Michael, Jesus is about to speak again."

"I am thirsty."

"Someone is offering Him a sponge soaked in vinegar on the end of a reed to drink."

"I think Jesus has taken it all; listen."

"It is finished."

"Michael, you can stand down. It's over. Jesus is about to say His final words."

"Father, into Your hands I commit My Spirit."

The Aftermath

After Jesus gave up His life, a series of miraculous events occurred. It was still dark when Jesus let out His final cry, and then the ground began to shake. Boulders and rocks split in two as some of the crowd ran back to the city.

In the temple, the curtain that separated the Holy of Holies (the earthly dwelling place of God's presence) from the rest of the temple split in two right down the middle.

The Father tore the veil.

After this, the graves of Old Testament saints who were sleeping opened, and many of them were raised to life and walked around in the holy city.

I recognized many of the saints and had a chance to speak with Lazarus.[23]

"Lazarus, can you give us a statement?"

"Well, the Lion of Judah has won the victory over the grave. He holds the keys of Death and Hades,[24] and we are all here to prove the power of His resurrection works."

While Mary and John and a few others were still standing near the cross, there was also a centurion standing by, observing everything taking place. After he realized what happened with the earthquake, all he could say was, "Surely He was the Son of God!"

Finally, it seemed what the people had done began to sink in—that they actually did put to death their Messiah. I realized this when I saw them beating their chests with conviction.

All this time the two criminals on either side of Jesus were still alive. Because the Jewish leaders didn't want their bodies to be left outside the gates of Jerusalem during Sabbath, they asked Pilate to have their legs broken.

---

23 Luke 16:22–23

24 Revelation 1:18

The soldiers broke the legs of both criminals, but when they came to Jesus, they found He was already dead. Then a soldier took a spear and plunged it into Jesus's side, and out flowed blood and water.

Later that day two of Jesus's followers who were in fact Pharisees, Joseph of Arimathea and Nicodemus, requested the body of Jesus from Pilate. With his permission they embalmed Jesus's body and laid Him in a tomb that had never been used before.

In a final attempt to ensure the disciples wouldn't have the opportunity to uncover the body of Jesus and then claim He resurrected of His own accord, the chief priests and Pharisees requested of Pilate that guards be set at the tomb for safekeeping.

He Is Risen

Early morning on the first day of the new week, Mary Magdalene and the other Mary arrived to view the tomb. I had since returned to heaven, but this trip was so much more joyful than my previous visit. It reminded me of when I first came to deliver the good news of Jesus's birth.

I had to cause a strong earthquake to loosen the stone at the entrance of the tomb and get the attention of the guards standing by. I rolled back the stone and sat on it. The soldiers standing guard were so amazed and shocked by my appearance (well, my clothes were white as snow, and my appearance was as lightning) that they went into shock and fell unconscious.

Then I spoke to the women. "Don't be afraid. I know you're looking for Jesus, who was crucified. He's not here; He is risen, just as He said. Come and see the place where He laid."

I showed them the empty tomb and the grave clothes neatly folded where His body had rested.

"Now hurry and let His disciples know; He has risen from the dead and is going ahead of you into Galilee. You will see Him there."

"This Same Jesus"

Jesus spent the last forty days appearing to various disciples and teaching them to go out into the world and preach the gospel. On His last encounter, five hundred disciples were gathered, whom He taught and told to wait in Jerusalem for the coming of the Comforter.

While He was talking with them, He ascended into heaven. When they couldn't see Him anymore because of the clouds, two friends of mine, dressed like myself, stood by them.

"Men of Galilee," they said, "why do you stand here looking into the sky? This same Jesus, who has been taken from you into heaven, will come back in the same way you have seen Him go."[25]

---

25 Acts 1:9

“Who’s Your Daddy?”

When Jesus returned to heaven, all the angels were gathered in the great hall of the throne room. We were clapping and smiling as He walked down toward the throne. He almost looked the same, but I could tell something was different. The scars from where He was nailed to the cross in His hands and feet were there. We were happy to see Him, but the scars reminded us of the sacrifice He made and the things He went through to redeem humankind.

“Hello, Gabriel.”

“It’s good to see You again, Jesus.”

“Thank you for your words in the garden … and for keeping the angels informed.”

I smiled, nodding my head. “Was it worth it?” I asked.

“You tell Me.”

Then Jesus looked over his shoulder, and I saw the criminal who repented on the cross standing at the door.

“The first of many?” I asked again.

“Absolutely,” Jesus replied, smiling.

Then He went up to the throne and sat down at the right hand of the Father.

“Welcome home, Son.”

“Thank You, Father.”

Then amid the cheering and clapping for the return of the Lamb of God, the heavenly Father spoke to His resurrected Son.

“My boy, my precious, precious boy …

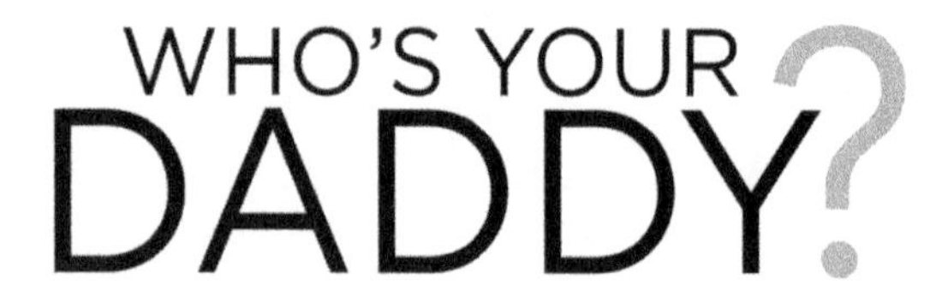

About the Author

This is the first collection of writings by Christian writer, David Robert Nelson. Born in Hackney, England, he spent his earlier years in northeast London. As a young teen, David migrated to Jamaica with his family.

It was in Jamaica that David accepted Christ as his Lord and Savior and has lived for the best part of thirty years serving in different departments of local churches. Having received a call from the Lord on his life, he returned to the UK, where he now resides in London with his wife, Lorna, and their sons, Da'lano and Jordan.

David fulfilled a lifetime dream of attending Spurgeon's College located in southeast London, where he successfully completed the "Equipped to Minister" course for lay pastors and preachers.

David is a Customer Service Officer for Southwark Council who sees his job of helping local residents as an extension of his ministry. Besides his local church, David is also an e-church member of the Potter's House, Dallas Texas.

Printed in the USA
CPSIA information can be obtained
at www.ICGtesting.com
JSHW022335140824
68134JS00019B/1503